MOM: SUPER-COOL, PRETTY, SECRET AGENT

By Kathy Long

For my husband, who always believes in me and works tirelessly to build me up. I always know you love me, "'Cause we're connected!"

ISBN: 9781796895155

Chapter 1

Scott sat patiently at the Waffle House, waiting on his contact to arrive and pass him the file he had been chasing for nearly a decade. This would finally make leaving the FBI worth it. He couldn't wait to see his cousin's face when he was the new media darling for exposing such a conspiracy. All he had to do was get the file. Once he had it, he knew that going public was the way to go. He even had a plan for someone to help with get the right media attention to make sure those involved couldn't escape. At least he hoped she would help. He hadn't asked her yet.

At eleven-thirty, Scott was more than concerned, as the meet was set for eleven. What could be keeping his contact? Maybe he is already here, Scott thought.

He scanned the room and noticed an older man with a ball cap and flannel shirt on. He was flirting way too much with the middle-aged waitress behind the counter. Her lipstick had faded, leaving her deep wrinkles pronounced against her dry, pale skin. Scott could see that she was becoming annoyed with his advances, and while he thought of intervening, he had more pressing needs at the moment. There was a business man in a suit in the booth nearest to the door.

He didn't have a briefcase or a computer. His clothes were pressed perfectly, and his shoes were freshly shined. Scott figured he must be going to a job interview, killing some time before it was due to start. No one else was in the restaurant. He had been stood up. All these years of work and chasing leads, of being thought of as a joke, and here he was about to make the case of a lifetime when he found himself once again empty-handed. Anger and regret welled up inside him.

Scott paid his tab and walked outside the building, cursing under his breath. As he started toward his car, a young man looking to be in his twenties approached Scott on his bicycle. It was clearly a mode of transportation for this man, not a hobby. He had his backpack strapped to the back and a sack of groceries hanging from the front handlebars. He was wearing ragged tennis shoes, dirty jeans and a "Pink Floyd" faded t-shirt. "Hey, Man, can you tell me how to get to the post office from here?" the man asked as he rocked back and forth slowly on the pedals of his bicycle to keep it upright.

"Not really, I'm here on vacation," Scott answered, trying to blow the man off. He was technically on vacation, but this was anything but a pleasure trip. He had come down from Virginia to follow the biggest lead of his life, and he had been stood up. He wasn't exactly in the mood to be helpful.

The man put his feet on the asphalt and pleaded "Come on, man. I've got this letter to mail, and –"

"I'm sorry. I can't help you," Scott interrupted, pushing past the man to his car.

The man rode his bike toward Scott's car and stopped on a dime. He grabbed Scott by the arm and spun him around. "Well, I can help you, brother. I've got just the thing for you. I think it's what you've been looking for," the man answered, "Don't forget to count your blessings."

"What?" Scott asked.

"Bless-ings," the man repeated slowly, staring right into Scott's eyes.

Scott wasn't sure what the man's game was, but he wasn't going to stick around to find out. Scott pulled away and opened his car door. He noticed an envelope under the windshield wipers and grabbed it as the man pedaled away on his bike. He had been expecting someone to meet him personally inside the restaurant, but perhaps his contact left the envelope? He ripped the envelope open to reveal something he didn't understand. There was a note paperclipped to some sort of flyer. "Follow the trail. Don't forget to count your blessings."

Scott looked up to see if his mystery biker was still in sight. He had to be the contact. But he needed more information. What trail? He was supposed to be getting a single file, not at trail. What blessings did he have to count? This certainly wasn't what was promised to him. Suddenly, he felt a sharp, quick pain in his stomach as a man came out of nowhere and stabbed him in the gut. Scott started to sink to the ground but fell into the car instead. From the color of the blood, he knew his time was short. He'd have to move up his timeline.

Chapter 2

Milk dripped from the granite countertop, splashing on the wooden chair leg on its way to the freshly mopped floor. Kate reached for the overturned glass and let out a muffled groan.

"Get your socks and shoes on!" she yelled from behind the counter, as if that was going to make her oldest son Landon move any faster. Plagued with ADHD and a propensity to push just the right buttons every morning, the lanky child had a knack for making things worse on an already bad morning. Kate longed for the days when she was just responsible to get herself to work on time, but only for moment. Her kids were a huge joy in her life despite the frustrations they brought. She grabbed a towel and started cleaning up the spilled milk. Landon was like a Tasmanian devil in the mornings – or at least a bull in a China cabinet -- and Kate was used to a routine that meant she would be cleaning something before heading out the door. Why couldn't he just sit and eat like he was told? Four minutes passed, and the blue-eyed redhead came bouncing back to the kitchen with bare feet holding a Pokémon card.

"Mom, Mom, I need to take this to show Sam! He doesn't have a Rock Ruff card."

"Landon. How many times have I asked you to get socks and shoes on?"

"But Mom--"

"Go!"

Landon squinted his blue eyes, gritted his teeth, and growled at his mother. Kate was unamused but decided not to vocalize her anger. Instead, she pointed to the den where Landon's socks and shoes lay undisturbed. He turned, seemingly unaffected by her gaze, and skipped without a care in the world toward his shoes. This time she followed him, standing over him as he tried to put the left shoe on his right foot.

"Landon, pay attention to what you are doing."

Landon let out a childlike laugh. "Oh yeah."

Kate smoothed his blonde hair against his head. "Let's go. We are late again."

"But I'm going to miss seeing Sam in line if we don't get there early."

"Then let's move it!" Landon sprinted to the door, shoes mostly tied. Kate grabbed her purse and lunch and followed Landon out the door. As usual, she had to grab his book bag and give it to him in the car.

"Oh yeah," he said, "thanks, Mom."

Kate mumbled under her breath, "Really? We are going to school. Why bother to take your book bag?!"

"Finally," grumbled a voice from the back seat. Logan. Always the people-pleasing child, ready to go to school. He was almost two years younger than Landon, but easily more mature than Landon. He was a normal-sized boy for his age, but he and Landon were the same size. His hair was slightly lighter than Landon's, and his eyes were green, but many people thought the two of them were twins for reasons unknown to Kate. She never had to worry about Logan following directions, unless his brother led him astray, and then the two of them could get into a lot of trouble. She worried about Logan being a teenager. He was eerily smart and manipulative even at his young age; she hated to think how good he would be at getting away with things later in life. He loved to joke and always marched to the beat of his own drum. Kate was still deciding if she should put him in to the gifted program at school or not. She didn't want him to be bored in regular classes, but she hated to see his childhood be robbed by all the insane projects that would surely take up all her family's free time. And she had enough on her plate with Landon. Somedays it was all she could do to get Landon to complete his homework without WWIII breaking out.

"Momma, what does the wind say at the end of the day?" Logan asked.

"I don't know, Logan, what does the wind say at the end of the day?" Kate responded.

"I blew it!" Logan answered with a grin.

"Very funny, Logan."

The two boys proceeded to laugh and talk to one another until their voices almost came to a scream. They got so excited in the car, just playing with one another. Kate couldn't understand the energy they had in the morning. "Hey, stopping yelling, you, two. You are right next to each other." Kate's words fell on deaf ears. She decided to focus her attention on the radio and try to drown them out with increasing volume, but again, she failed.

The black Pontiac rounded the corner into the school parking lot and came to a screeching halt. The line was longer than usual this morning. Were they really that late? Kate hoped she could still make it to work on time. As they creeped forward, Landon spotted his friend Sam. He rolled the window down and hung his head out, screaming at the top of his lungs at his friend from across the lot. Kate quickly weighed her options – let it go or make him roll up the window? Thoughts of what her parents would do flashed in her head, but she dismissed it. She didn't want to have another fight this morning. And, she rationalized, what exactly was it hurting to let her child be loud in the parking lot? She turned the song on the local Christian station up a notch again and caught Logan mouthing the words in the rear-view mirror. She smiled, happy with her influence on him toward Christian music. Eventually, they made it to the front of the line.

"Bye, Mom – love you!" Logan shouted hurriedly as he slammed the door, not waiting for a response. She had long given up on a goodbye kiss. One of Logan's quirks was that he would give hugs, but never a kiss. Kate found it strange that her son didn't like "mommie kisses". She could understand when he got older, but he had refused him since age four. What four-year-old doesn't like "mommie kisses"?

Landon exited with the same speed, once again leaving his book bag behind. Kate rolled her window down and shouted, "Aren't you forgetting something, Landon?"

"Oh yeah," he said, reaching into her car window to hug her and planting a kiss on her cheek.

"Very sweet, Landon." It wasn't what she meant, but a kiss from an 8-year-old was always welcome, especially given the frustration he had caused earlier. She handed him the book bag and watched them enter the building.

Kate headed to work. She pushed the radio buttons frantically, searching for just the right song. Kate had always loved music, and there was nothing like 30 minutes in the car by herself singing along to the radio. Lately she had been listening to songs from her youth – hard rock and glam metal that most people considered anything but music. She scanned the dial, stopping on "Hair Nation". She loved that silly music – the guitars, the drums – it was fun. It reminded her of her school days, but she knew how toxic the words really were. That music had become her secret vice. Even though she probably had heard the song playing a couple hundred times, she didn't even know the verses. Only the chorus. And every lick of the guitar solo. Could it really be all that bad if she didn't know the words? She decided if she was asking that question, she should probably not listen to it. She turned it back to a Christian station and found one of her favorite songs playing. She tapped on the steering wheel and sang the words loudly all the way to work despite her lack of singing talent. It was her 30 minutes, and she planned to enjoy it!

Kate pulled into the lot at 7:56, grabbing the last space available. She slammed the car in park and ran upstairs as the arthritis in her knee made her cringe with every step. Plopping in her chair by 7:58, she thought to herself, "Made it." She checked her email to find the inbox empty and wondered why it was so important to everyone she be here at exactly 8:00 am when there was nothing for her to do. After 20 years in marketing, Kate had finally found a job that didn't require more of her than she could produce. There were no after-hours emergencies, no checking email all night long, and no office drama. It was by far the least stressful job she had ever had, and yet for some reason, one of the most difficult. She had been told in her interview that Marketing would never be a focus for this manufacturing company, but she certainly didn't realize how little she'd be responsible for doing. She had started out like every job, assessing the market, providing a strategic plan as she saw it for the marketing efforts only to realize that this job was anything but strategic. She tried plotting tactics and budgets, but in the end, everything was done on a one-off basis to satisfy the current whims of the leadership and rarely had anything to do with her ideas. It was an unusual industry, and whatever she did wasn't going to move the needle of sales either way. Truth be told, they really needed a part-time specialist at a third of her salary to execute tactics they deemed necessary. She felt mostly useless in her job, sometimes even inadequate. She was fairly certain most of the office viewed her as a mere administrative assistant to the sales director, her boss Jim.

Ironically, Jim was the one person in the company who thought she had a brain and didn't view her as an administrator. He was quickly enamored with her seeming intellect when he learned she was a Georgia Tech graduate. At first, he thought of her more as an equal, but he quickly realized that after 25 years of not using any of her math and engineering skills, she was anything but an equal in terms of math. But they had other conversations. Daily encounters with Jim were fun when they didn't discuss work, but any mention of anything related to the job at hand left Kate feeling downright stupid. As an overachiever, it was a hard pill to swallow.

Kate's day began as uneventful as usual. She proceeded with the few reports she was responsible to send out, then checked her personal email and finance accounts, looking for anything to occupy her brain for the duration of the day. She grabbed her iphone and texted her mom to check in, a friend to say hi, her husband to blow him a kiss. No responses. Everyone else was clearly busy, which is exactly what Kate was supposed to be...busy! Doing something useful. Something that mattered. And yet here she was, stuck staring at an empty inbox wasting her talents. She surfed the news sites for anything that captured her attention and then moved on to her online Bible devotional for the day. She could at least be spiritually productive, she thought.

And then there it was, another twinge from her gut as she read silently the words from the Apostle Paul: "Do everything without grumbling or arguing, so that you may become blameless and pure children of God without fault in a warped and crooked generation." Here was Paul, imprisoned for nothing but sharing the Good News of Jesus with others, and he managed to rejoice and sing praises to God for his situation, not in spite of it. Could she really be grumbling over a job where her only real responsibility was to just show up and be available? Do everything without grumbling. What about grumbling about doing nothing? Kate was sure that fell into the same arena. She knew she had work to do on her attitude. When had she fallen off the wagon on being grateful? Well, it was certainly time to get back on it, she thought.

The iphone buzzed with a text. Finally, human interaction. Kate punched in her password and read the text from her mom: "Don't forget Landon's evaluation today at school". She had forgotten. But suddenly she was overjoyed. She had asked permission to leave work early to go to the evaluation and spend a few minutes with the kids. What a great treat! She finished the rest of her shortened work day thinking about doing everything without grumbling.

14

Kate grabbed her purse and lunch bag and headed down the stairs. Down was harder on her knee than up, and she usually grabbed onto the handrail and held the wall as she descended. Once she reached the bottom, she proceeded out the door. "Going to my kids' school for a meeting. I'll be back tomorrow," she mentioned to the receptionist on the way out.

Chapter 3

Kate entered the school parking lot and pulled her car into the next to the last aisle where no one else was parked. She could have parked closer, but she didn't want to have to search for a spot and be late. She entered the school office and announced her meeting to the receptionist who showed her to the conference room. She was there to discuss the latest evaluation on her oldest son's progress regarding his ADHD. She always dreaded these meetings, wondering who was taking note of her parenting style. It always seemed that the to-do list started and ended with her needing to do more to help Landon. It was harder than she had imagined having a child with ADHD, mostly because she couldn't understand his struggles and didn't know where the ADHD stopped and Landon began. She had a hard time accepting that ADHD was real at first. Landon just seemed like a kid with a lot of energy and lack of drive. It was difficult for Kate to understand that you couldn't just make him finish his work. He struggled with processing time, and visually things overwhelmed him. He had behavior problems at times, but not enough to get him into trouble at school. He mostly wanted control at home, and Kate often butted heads with him. She tried to do the strategies that were suggested, but it seemed to be a never-ending battle with little forward progress. What hurt her so much was that Landon was such a bright, funny child, and she didn't know how to help him not struggle.

Poor Logan, he never got any help or attention. Whatever guilt she felt about not being able to help Landon achieve his full potential was equal to the guilt of paying too much attention to Landon and not enough to Logan.

Kate entered the large conference room and waited patiently for the meeting to start. Everything about this room wreaked of money, something that didn't make much sense in a public school. The brown chairs were leather, the table was carved mahogany, and the walls were much more like a museum than a school. Kate wondered what stay-home mom's family donated the money for this room. She felt sick just thinking about how inadequate she was at work and as a mom, and jealousy filled her for those parents who could afford for the mom to stay home. Suddenly, Kate became consumed by thoughts of other parents and how she didn't measure up. She listened half-heartedly to the list of action items that the psychologist gave her, wondering when she might squeeze these in after work.

At the end of the meeting, Kate exited the lavish conference area and re-entered the regular school office area, which was still abuzz with parents, teachers, and kids, all asking for something from the frazzled receptionist. The buses were leaving campus, but the kids with stay-home moms who couldn't fathom their children riding the bus home lined in the hallway and were creating quite a ruckus. Kate signed her kids out and quickly scanned the area for her children. Logan was easy to spot – the largest kid in first grade, and the only one sitting quietly as he was told. He was the rule-follower, and Kate loved him for that. Landon, on the other hand, appeared to be leading a group of boys in playing some sort of game he had made up. She chuckled to herself at his imagination and ability to convince others to follow along despite his small size. She motioned to Landon and said, "Time to go, Landon. Say goodbye to your friends."

"Not yet," Landon said, turning his back on her and continuing to play the game.

Infuriated but not surprised with his disrespectful attitude, Kate quickly grabbed Landon by the hand as he protested and pulled backward.

"Time to go, Landon. Say goodbye to your friends." Kate repeated, slightly more aggravated than before.

"But we're not finished yet!" Landon whined.

"Time to go," Kate sternly said, yanking his hand so hard his body lunged forward out of the crowd. Whoops. In her anger, Kate forgot how lightweight he was. Weight had always been a problem in her family. For Kate, it as being too heavy her whole life, but for Landon, it was the opposite problem. He was skinny and a very picky eater. He would rather play than finish any meal or snack. It was hard for Kate to imagine; someone that could eat whatever they wanted and stay not just slim, but very skinny. Enough where it seemed necessary to put rocks in his pocket to keep the wind from blowing him away.

Logan sensed what was happening and quickly moved toward her undetected, wanting to be recognized as being the good child. Kate spun around to call out to Logan, but he was already there. She nearly knocked him over from the force of the turn.

"Hi, Momma!" Logan bellowed out, grabbing her free hand and giving her a huge smile.

"Hi, Logan! How was your day?" she asked gleefully.

"It was awesome. I want to show—"

"I want to play with my friends," shouted Landon.

"Not now, Landon. It's time to go home. And don't interrupt your brother" Kate snapped.

"You never let me play. You always make me leave early. I'm not going." Landon pouted, planting his feet. Kate was rarely able to come to school, much less to pick up the kids. They certainly weren't leaving early, but rational thought no longer was in play. In Kate's experience with Landon, there was no way to convince him to the contrary, so she decided not to play his game.

"Landon, it's time to go home." She said firmly, hoping her response would elicit compliance.

"No, it's not. Evan doesn't have to leave yet. Why can't I stay with him?"

Kate could feel the anger boiling inside her while the crowd watched her, judged her. She let go of Logan's hand and bent down to face Landon. She whispered sternly, "I'm not going to say it again. We are leaving." Landon could sense her anger but was unmoved by it. He walked with his head down all the way to the car, tears welling up in his eyes.

Kate unlocked the doors and approached the car. A white Honda had parked way too close to her, making a quick getaway nearly impossible. She tried not to door ding the car, but there wasn't enough room for the smallest of people, let alone someone her size. She held her breath as the door bumped the other car. Horrified, she noticed the driver was still inside, and he was staring right at her. "Sorry," she mouthed, being more irritated at the bad parking job of the other driver than sorry for the ding. She hoped he wouldn't make a scene. After all, he was the one parked over the line. Her heart raced a little as he exited the car and stumbled to the passenger side, as if to assess any damage. The man looked to be in his late 40s and clearly wasn't prepared to pick up his children at school. She wasn't sure if he was drunk or on drugs, but the look in his eyes told him he wasn't in the best state of mind. And he appeared to be sweating even though he had on a hoodie and a coat. It was 45 degrees outside. Great, he's probably a mean drunk, Kate thought. She winced slightly as he approached her, bracing herself for what was to come.

The man stepped close to the open door, pressing it against Kate as he stumbled forward. He pushed a folded piece of paper around the side of the door, offering it to Kate. She looked down at the folded paper, thinking it was probably his insurance information. Kate didn't think she did that much damage, but she didn't want to get on the wrong side of this man who was obviously having a bad day. She hesitantly reached for it. As her fingers closed around the paper and started to unfold it, he whispered, "blessings," and walked away from the cars. It was then that Kate noticed it wasn't a stumble but a limp. Confused, relieved, and anxious to get away from an awkward confrontation, Kate quickly squeezed into the car and read the paper. It was a flyer offering a discount at the local trampoline place. She tossed it aside and started out of the lot, thankful for the nice gesture.

Landon took the opportunity to gain back Kate's attention. "You're the worst mommie ever. You never let me play," He gruffed.

Kate had learned a long time ago that her son's outbursts were related to the ADHD and were not rational. She knew not to take it personally, but that rarely stopped her own self-doubt about her ability as a mother from creeping up to the surface. So much for a fun afternoon with the kids.

Chapter 4

After dinner, Kate took a minute to sit on her bed and read a news story. Before she could get to the meat of the story, in came Landon who hopped on the bed and started their regular game of "Tackle Mom". Kate played along and let Landon knock her over. She grabbed him tight for a hug, laughed and kissed him furiously on the cheek until he started cackling.

"You are my little redheaded tiger!" Kate playfully joked with him.

"Grrrr! I'm a baby red tiger!" Landon insisted as he got up on all fours on her stomach and pawed gently at his mom.

"Get up, Momma! It's my turn to knock you down!" Logan shouted. Kate pushed Landon off her playfully and sat back up on the bed. She put her arms up to defend against the would-be tackler as Logan ran toward the bed.

"I'll help you, Logan. I'm a red tiger!" Landon shouted from behind as he grabbed Kate's shoulders to help bring her down. Kate again relinquished control and fell back on the bed as if the boys had managed to tackle her.

The playing went on for several minutes, each time with all three of them laughing loudly and escalating the fun. It was Kate's favorite time of the day.

The timer dinged, indicating playtime was over and it was time for bed. After a little whining, Kate and Jason managed to get the kids in bed, help with their covers and say goodnight at least 3 times to each kid. Finally, the lights were out, and all was quiet. It was only 9 pm, but Kate was exhausted. She plopped on the couch next to her husband and sighed.

Jason was a man out of time – one that longed for the simple life with his family. Nothing much rattled his cage, and even less got him excited, which was strange given that he was a true redhead. He had a temper; it just took a long time to activate it. Jason was a calm, gentle balance to Kate's insane pace.

"I'm worried about Landon not taking anything seriously. Do I play with them too much when I should be making them learn something?"

"Relax, Kate. They are little boys. One day they will grow out of playtime, and you'll treasure these memories. You are a good mother. Just enjoy the ride."

She loved how Jason always seemed to know exactly the right thing to say. He was a man of few words, but when he spoke, his words meant something.

"Oh, I got something today. Maybe we can take the boys Saturday," she said, jumping up to go back to the kitchen to retrieve the flyer. "I went to pick up the boys today at school, and some guy parked way too close to me. I door dinged him and thought he was going to be mad at me, but instead he gave me this buy-one-get-one free coupon and said, 'blessings'. It was so weird. Anyway, do you want me to get the tickets, so we can take the boys this Saturday?"

"Sure. What time?" Jason replied, half listening and half hoping it would be when he was busy with his MAG group. Jason had become involved in what Kate could only describe as a redneck cult; a group of ex-military men and women who were all prepping for the apocalypse. MAG stood for Mutual Assistance Group. They continually took stock of what was in their "go bag" in case they had to "bug out" and survive in the wilderness or a secluded location. Kate thought it was weird, but harmless, as they only met up once a month to go hiking or camping, run communication drills, or have target practice. Kate was happy Jason had some friends, even if they were a little strange.

"Let's see." Kate flipped open her ipad and started to type in the web address. "That's funny," she giggled. "No one uses a proofreader anymore. They misspelled their own website on the flyer. Look. They spelled it xdrenlaine.com. rather than xdrenaline.com."

Kate typed in the corrected address in the search bar and proceeded to try to buy tickets for "open jump" using the promo code listed. Her efforts resulted in the error "promo code not active." She tried again to no avail. "Well, that's frustrating. The coupon says it is good through next week."

Jason looked over, listening half to her and half to the earbud in his ear. His ham radio was full of static this time of night, but he insisted on listening, just in case he heard something interesting. Kate thought it was way too much like police scanning or a verbal chat room for her taste. It was hard to understand how listening to a bunch of old men talk about their fishing trip, traffic or the weather could be fun, but she didn't say much about it anymore. "Maybe they didn't spell the website wrong on the flyer," Jason offered.

"That doesn't make any sense. The name of the place is Xdren-a-line – we've been there before. Why would their website be Xdren-laine? I'm on the site now. It's not like there would be two websites for the same place." Kate was dismissive in her response, and immediately felt badly for her harsh tone. She decided to rectify the situation by humoring her husband. She typed in xdrenlaine.com but knew deep down she was doing it more to prove herself right than make it up to her husband. The ipad churned for a moment, but just as Kate started to gloat internally, the site loaded. She assumed the company had bought both domains and had the misspelled address routed to the correct one. But the menu was different, and some of the items were misspelled.

"This is weird." Kate was truly perplexed, but Jason had gone back to his radio and was oblivious to what she was doing.

"KN4CQJ," he called out, waiting for a response.

Kate rolled her eyes at his dorky hobby. She double-checked the web address and noted that the site had not rerouted back to the original site. She proceeded to go through the process of buying the tickets again, using the promo code on the flyer. She thought it was a strange error but was interested in making up for today with the kids by taking them somewhere fun. A popup appeared asking her to verify her email address. Kate hated when companies made you provide your email address, as they were relentless about follow up promotional emails. But she wanted to make it up to her kids more. She entered her email address and clicked the link when it appeared. The page prompted, "Enter your password."

"Uugh!" Kate let out a frustrating growl and slammed the ipad shut. She grabbed the remote and flipped the TV on, clicking to something recorded on her DVR.

Jason was unaffected by her emotional outburst. He had become accustomed to her melodrama. He pushed the radio down beside him on the couch to not draw her attention to it, but he wasn't giving up listening while they watched one of her chick-flick shows.

Half-way through the program, Kate grabbed the ipad again. She hadn't heard a word of the dialogue on the program since the beginning. Her brain had churned non-stop over this coupon. This silly coupon. Part of Kate's charm was her relentless pursuit of knowledge. She had to question everything, analyze everything, and ultimately drive everyone around her mad. And yet, it was as if she couldn't control it. Why didn't that link work? What password? Why would a coupon ask for a password? And why was there a second website? Why did that guy give her a coupon in the first place? Did he work there? She had to know. Kate tried both websites again, going through the same motions as before, with the exact same results.

"What password? Why would I have a password for a coupon?" Kate yelled at the ipad.

"Kate." Jason interrupted.

"What?" she answered and looked back down at the ipad. "I-don't-have-a-password" she barked at the ipad slowly, as if it was listening.

"Kate. It's a coupon."

"I know, but why doesn't it work? Why do businesses do this? Why would I need a password for a coupon?"

"Not everyone can be a perfectionist like you. They made a mistake."

"But that's a hard mistake to make. First, there are two websites. And second, you have to create a secure page only accessible by a password. You don't do that by mistake."

"Well, maybe there is a super-secret password only the stay-home moms know," Jason said with a smile, knowing it get a laugh and get under Kate's skin at the same time.

Kate lightly chuckled and closed the ipad again. She tried once again to focus on the television to no avail. She was so lost in thought that she forgot to fast forward through the commercials. Jason certainly didn't notice. He was engrossed in listening to the static in his right ear. Suddenly, Kate remembered that she hadn't even looked at whatever Logan wanted to show her. She had become so involved in the argument with Landon and the door ding incident that once again Logan had been left out. He had not mentioned whatever it was he wanted to show her again. She needed to remember to ask him about it tomorrow, but she knew it would be too late. The damage was done. Logan had been cast to the side once again, and she wanted to make it up to him. Logan loved trampoline parks. There had to be a way to get his coupon. She opened the ipad a third time and clicked the link provided to her email once again. She started typing random words in the password box: BOGO, KIDS, COUPON, FREE. All of them registered an error. Then she remembered the man's word when he gave her the coupon. BLESSINGS. She typed it in, and a pop-up appeared. "Thank you. You'll receive an email shortly."

"Really? It's a coupon you people. Just let me buy the tickets already." Kate yelled at the ipad, again as if it could hear her. She slammed the ipad cover closed and went to bed.

Chapter 5

Kate hit the snooze for the second time on her phone, dreading getting out of bed so early. She pushed the covers off and started to roll out of bed. She got to her feet and heard the popping noises in her ankles ramp up as she headed toward the kids' rooms. Jason had been up and gone before her alarm chirped, so she was on her own again this morning.

She leaned down over Logan and kissed him. It was the only time she could steal a kiss without being blocked. "Stop it, Momma!" He yelled.

"Get up, sleepy head. Time for school!" Kate said as cheerfully as she could muster. Logan still loved school. First grade was exciting and full of fun activities. He enjoyed the interaction with others and loved the praise he got from teachers for doing a good job. Kate hoped that learning would continue to be this fun for him as he grew older.

Logan rolled over. He put his knees under him and his head on the pillow. "Will you turn on the light, and then I'll get up?"

Kate complied and then went to Landon's room to see him sitting straight up in the bed with a big goofy grin on his face. Landon was a morning person and seemed always to be awake before anyone else. She wondered how he functioned with so much energy every day, but she was like that as a teenager and young adult. She remembered having insomnia most nights and just didn't require a lot of sleep. "Ready for a ride, red tiger?" Kate asked Landon.

Landon pawed at Kate like a tiger and shook his head yes. Kate walked over to the bed and picked Landon up on her back and carried him to the den. She put him down on the floor in front of the couch and hugged him. Landon was way more affectionate than Logan and loved to kiss his mom. Kate enjoyed about thirty seconds of hugs and kisses with Landon before announcing it was time to get clothes on.

Landon protested slightly with another hug, but Kate pulled his pajamas off quickly and handed him clothes. She got up from the couch as Logan yelled, "My turn! My turn!"

Kate made her way back to Logan's room and agreed to give him a piggy back ride. She pulled him around the den and spun to a stop, nearly falling onto the couch because of his size. "Again! Again!" Logan shouted.

"No, one is enough. We have to get ready for school, and I need a shower," Kate insisted as Logan groaned. She noticed Landon had managed to do nothing in the time she had been gone from the room. "Come on, Landon. Today is Friday. You know what that means, right?"

"Oh yeah!" Landon shouted with glee. "I get to turn the computers on! Come on, Logan. I can't be late today! Today is Tech Crew Day. I get to turn the computers on in the media center."

"No fair," Logan said. "Momma, when can I do that?"

"Logan, you can do it when you are in third grade like me," Landon said, putting his clothes on in a hurry for a change.

"Ok, get dressed, Logan. I'll go get your breakfast ready," Kate said. "And then I have to take a shower."

Kate walked back to the kitchen and grabbed two bowls from the cabinet, careful to choose the same color so that her kids wouldn't fight over the bowls. She grabbed some instant oatmeal from the pantry along with the Fruit Spins and begin to fill the bowls. She moved to the microwave and put some water in to heat while she grabbed the milk from the refrigerator and poured milk on the cereal. She pulled the water from the microwave and added it to the oatmeal, stirring it to just the right consistency Landon liked and sat both bowls at their places. She put the milk back and grabbed a protein shake for Landon as she started out of the kitchen to the shower. "Breakfast is ready. Get it eaten before I get dressed, or we won't make it in time for the technology crew, Landon."

Usually, Kate couldn't trust her kids to eat breakfast while she did other things. They got distracted and played at the table more than they ate. But today,

Landon had a mission and that always motivated him to get ready on time. She hopped in the shower and finished getting fully dressed before emerging from the bedroom. She was pleasantly surprised to see Landon had eaten all his breakfast and had left the table. Logan was still working on the cereal, but he seemed close to being complete. Kate checked the time and saw that they had a window of 5-10 minutes before they needed to leave.

"Landon. Teeth. Have you brushed?" No answer. "Landon? Teeth!" Again, no answer. Kate looked at Logan and said, "Ok, hurry and go brush your teeth so we can go."

Kate wondered into the bathroom where she hoped Landon was brushing his teeth. She wasn't surprised to see him playing with a toy dinosaur on the messy counter. She grabbed his toothbrush and put toothpaste on it.

"That's Logan's toothbrush," he argued.

"Ok, where is your toothbrush?" she asked.

Landon pulled out the drawer and pointed with the dinosaur at a blue toothbrush. Kate reached to grab it, and Landon yelled, "No, let Scruffles get it."

"Tell Scruffles to hurry. You need to be done with this and putting your shoes on," Kate said as Landon slowly pretended to let the dinosaur pull his toothbrush out of the drawer. Kate tried to wait patiently, but she couldn't. She grabbed the toothbrush out of Landon's hands and started to put toothpaste on it. "Brush," she said. Landon squished his nose and took the toothbrush reluctantly as he stared at her. "Brush," she repeated. Landon began brushing his teeth slowly.

"Logan!" Kate yelled just as Logan entered the room.

"What, Momma?"

Kate grabbed the toothbrush she had already put toothpaste on and handed it to Logan. "Brush," she said.

"But I don't like this kind of toothpaste. It's sour. That's Landon's toothpaste," Logan said.

Frustrated, Kate said, "Too bad, so sad. Just brush, Logan. Landon, finish."

Landon spit hard into the sink, splattering toothpaste everywhere, including on the mirror. Kate rolled her eyes and wanted to smack him in the back of the head. Instead she grabbed the toothbrush from him and said, "Go get your shoes on so we can go. Tonight, when you get home, you can clean your bathroom."

Kate turned just in time to see Logan finish wiping the toothpaste off his brush onto the counter. "Logan, what are you doing?"

"That's not my toothpaste," he said, wiping the last bit off his toothbrush.

Kate snatched the toothbrush. "It's toothpaste, Logan. Why would you wipe it on the counter?" Kate asked in a shrill voice. Logan's stare was blank. "We don't wipe toothpaste on the counter. Brush your teeth. I'm leaving in 3 minutes with or without you," Kate said loudly.

Kate walked into the den where she hoped Landon was putting on his shoes. Instead, she saw him in the kitchen under the table playing with his dinosaur. "Landon, shoes," she said in a huff. Landon ignored her. How had the morning come unraveled so quickly? Kate walked over to the table and snatched Landon by the arm. "Shoes. Now!"

Chapter 6

Kate pulled into the lot again at 7:56 am. She just couldn't seem to get there any earlier with dropping the kids off at school. She headed inside and nearly collided with Barbara in the hall. Barbara was the receptionist/billing assistant. She was an odd lady who made everyone else's business her own. She had strawberry blonde hair that was thinning on top and wore glasses to read that were always hanging around her neck. She had taken a liking to Kate, probably because Kate chose to let things slide that drove others crazy.

"Oh, sorry, I'll try not to knock you down next time," she said with a smile, hoping Barbara wouldn't put her on her "bad list." Kate knew she had one. She was always gossiping about others and making life difficult for those on her list. Kate wanted to avoid that list at all cost.

"You are like Road Runner blazing through here," Barbara huffed.

Kate wondered what column that put her into on Barbara's list. "Yeah, I'm sorry. It's dropping the kids off. It's making me nearly late," Kate whined, hoping to play on Barbara's sympathy.

"Kids. What are you gonna do?" Barbara replied. "Oh, some guy called for you yesterday while you were gone." Kate really didn't care. No one ever called her unless they were selling something, but still, she needed to make Barbara feel needed to stay in her good graces.

"Oh yeah? Did he tell you what he wanted?" Kate asked, uninterested in the answer.

"No, he was kind rude and talked all like a heavy breather. It was creepy. He said it was really important he talk to you, but then he hung up on me when I told him you had to go to your kids' school."

"Ok, thanks. Probably that guy from Staples. He is always calling me with some emergency sale of stuff I don't need. Maybe he got the message, huh? Well, off to work. See ya," Kate waved as she started up the stairs.

"Later, chickie," Barbara called out.

Fridays at work meant Kate had something to do. Well, at least for the first 45 minutes or so. She was responsible for reports and a PowerPoint for the weekly status meeting. She had instructions on how to create the reports and slides but had no real understanding of what the numbers and charts meant. She followed the instructions to the letter, making a game of how fast she could complete the mundane task. She found it a waste of time, as no one sitting more than 2 feet from the screen could see the numbers, and only about 3 people in the room knew what they meant. Kate wanted to revamp the meeting and produce slides that told the story of what was going on in a way everyone could understand. Big picture status updates from each department, action items for others – these were the things that made meetings useful, not an hour and a half of staring at tiny numbers on a screen. But as one of only four women in the building, and certainly the least respected, she kept her thoughts to herself and plugged away at the assignment at hand.

Kate glanced toward the phone on her right; the message light was blinking. Odd, she hadn't noticed it when she came in, and usually the telemarketers didn't start calling until mid-morning. Kate punched in the password and listened with her finger on the "9" key, anxious to delete the message as soon as she could verify that it was another telemarketer. She grabbed her pencil and with the free hand, just in case it was one she would be passing along to her boss – a misdial. It seemed silly to her that she would get so excited about a misdial, but it was an opportunity to do something – anything – and often just delivering a message meant she could get part of the assignment for resolution. She listened closely, but she was met with only silence for 8 seconds. A misdial for sure. Kate wondered why they didn't hang up faster, but her curiosity quickly turned to irritation as she deleted the non-message.

"Do everything without complaining," she reminded herself. Kate decided it was time to get back in the Word again. Today's lesson was in Corinthians. Paul again. She loved Paul's writings, but some were difficult to swallow. She read the passage but found that her mind wandered off mid-way through, focusing instead on the long list of action items she had received at Landon's evaluation meeting yesterday. Instead of stopping to reread the passage, Kate figured it would be best to try again after lunch. Lunch. She had forgotten to grab it on the way out the door. She was beginning to wonder if she was the one with ADHD rather than Landon.

Kate started down the stairs, hands on both walls. Her arthritic-stricken knee wasn't too fond of going down. She heard the pops and cracks as she descended, hoping no one would come behind her, forcing her to move faster. She came to the bottom of the stairs and headed for the door. She braced herself for the cold as she pushed the door open. The sun was brighter than she anticipated, and she found herself closing her eyes for every two out of three steps. She walked around the corner to her car when a hand grabbed her arm from behind. Startled, she flung herself around and tried to snatch her arm back. The grip was fierce, and she was unable to break free. Terrified, Kate slung her other arm toward the man who had ahold of her, but he blocked her wild punch and grabbed her wrist and turned her around. Her forehead slammed into the car, and the man pressed the front of her body hard against it. She felt something hard against her back. Kate picked up her foot ready to stomp his, but she couldn't see where his feet were. She stomped twice, missing both times as he whispered harshly, "Stop! I'm not going to hurt you; just give me the file."

"File? What file?" Kate screeched. "I don't know what you are talking about. Let me go!" she shouted as she tried once again to break free and stomp her assailant's foot backwards. She had watched hundreds of movies where the wimpy woman let a man over power her. She was determined not to be that woman. She was smarter than all those dumb women on television, and while not muscular, she certainly was not frail. She knew that if he were to get her away from here, her chance of survival would be less than 1%. Kate knew he couldn't carry her even if he managed to knock her out. She was determined; if he meant her harm, he'd have to kill her here. In the parking lot. In the middle of the day.

"I know he gave it to you yesterday. Just give me the file, and we are done."

"Let me go!" Kate barked back. She put her foot on the car door and pushed off the car hard enough to knock both of them off balance and onto the ground. He landed with a thud of his head and groaned as Kate landed on top of his stomach, her weight squishing him into the asphalt. Kate rolled to her right and pushed upward with all fours. She caught the glimpse of a something shiny on his hip as she reached for her key. She managed to unlock the car and climb inside before the man recovered from the fall. She quickly backed out of the space and headed for the exit as her assailant jumped to his feet. As if he thought she would stop, the man threw his arms in the air and jumped in front of the car. Kate swerved to miss him but got a good look at his face, as well as a holstered weapon and a badge. Kate sped out of the lot unsure of what had just happened or what to do next.

Chapter 7

Kate drove a mile down the road toward town, intending to go straight to the police station. Why would a cop attack me? What file does he want? Is he a dirty cop? Why me? Kate's head buzzed with a host of other questions. She slammed the radio dial off so she could concentrate. She needed to call Jason and go to the police. She dug into her purse but couldn't find her phone. Kate was afraid to pull over; at least while she was moving she felt safe, but she needed that phone. She drove toward the police station and continued unsuccessfully to dig in her purse for the phone as she drove. As she pulled into the station lot, she was overcome with fear that the man who attacked her was a dirty cop and worked out of this precinct. Should she go in? Oh, where was that phone! She needed to call Jason or 9-1-1.

Kate parked the car but left it running. She thought for a moment, "Be smart about this. You've seen a ton of movies and television shows where the character does the wrong thing. Don't do that." She was afraid to close her eyes, but knew she needed Jesus to help her.

"Lord, tell me what to do!" she pleaded. "I am trying not to grumble through this, but I really need your help here." Humor always made her feel better. She hoped God would see it that way.

Kate scanned the parking lot. She hadn't seen any new cars since she arrived, which meant if her assailant was a dirty cop working out of here, he was well behind her. He probably figured she would come here first, as that makes the most sense for a victim. She'd have to be on guard. But getting the police involved was the only logical step. Kate made one last sweep of her purse for the phone. After coming up empty, she decided going in was the only way out. She exited the car and walked swiftly inside, fully aware of her surroundings.

Fortunately, Kate worked in a small town outside the city where a police precinct wasn't too crowded on a Friday afternoon. She walked toward the front desk as a woman on the bench at the door hollered out something inaudible her way. Kate pressed on. There was only one officer working the desk, and he was busy handing a belligerent man, arguing about paperwork. Kate was unsure what the issue was, and it didn't much matter to her. What mattered was that she needed help. She waited, shifting her weight back and forth to avoid pain in her knee as the officer and patron continued to battle. She wasn't sure how long she should wait around but wasn't sure where else to go either. Finally, the man yelled an obscenity at the officer and walked off. "Thank you, Lord," Kate thought as she approached the desk. The officer looked down at his paperwork and uttered a simple, "Yes," without even looking at Kate.

Kate wasn't even sure where to begin or what to say. She paused.

"How can I help you, ma'am?" The officer asked as he continued staring down at his paperwork.

"Um," Kate began, "I'm not entirely sure."

The officer started with a sarcastic tone, "Well, if you aren't sure, then I'm pretty sure I can't help you." The officer looked up from the paperwork to Kate's flushed face, her hands trembling. His gaze softened and forced a smile, "Ma'am, you have to tell me something in order for me to be able to help you."

Kate brushed her long red locks out of her face and took a deep breath. She was overcome with emotion and tears started to fall from her green eyes. She spoke quickly and without taking another breath. "I left for lunch and a man grabbed me and tried to attack me. He said he wouldn't hurt me if I gave him the file, but I don't know what file he is talking about and he had a gun and – "

"Slow down, ma'am; just take a breath!"

"I can't. This man, he wanted a file from me, but I don't know what he is talking about. And he had a gun and a badge. Why would a cop –"

"A gun and a badge? The man that attacked you had a gun AND a badge?" the officer asked, clearly not believing Kate's description.

"Yes, that's what I'm saying. He grabbed me in the parking lot and shoved me against the car and –"

"Are you sure he had a badge?" the officer asked yet again.

"Yes, a badge. And a gun. And he wanted a file from me."

"What file, ma'am?" The sarcasm turned to cynicism in his voice.

"I don't know. I-I-I don't have a file. I'm a marketing manager. I'm just a wife and a mother. Why would anyone think I had a file? I need to call my husband. Can I use your phone?"

"Ma'am let's start at the beginning. What is your name?"

The door to the precinct slammed shut, catching Kate's attention. She whirled around to see another uniformed officer walking toward the desk. Her nametag read "YATES." She couldn't be but about 90lbs soaking wet. Her radio blared, "That's a negative. I no longer have a 20 on that suspect. I'm proceeding to the house."

Kate looked past the officer to see an unmarked car arrive. She wasn't sure, but the driver could have been her assailant. What if it was? Surely, he wouldn't attack her again inside the police department. She was safe in here, right? Right. She turned back to the officer and started again, "I think the man that attacked me was a cop."

"Ok, hold on there, ma'am. That's a pretty serious charge you are making. We don't take that stuff lightly. I'm sure what you saw was something else."

"I know what I saw, and he had a badge and a gun." Kate was furious that he would question what she saw.

"I tell you what. Let's take a minute. Officer Yates, can you take this woman and get her some water?"

"No," Kate protested. "I need to call my husband. Can I use your phone?"

"I'm sorry ma'am, but the phones are for business use only. Officer Yates can take your statement in this room over here." The officer pointed to a small corner office with 2 extra chairs.

Kate entered the room hesitantly, scanning for an extra exit in case she needed it. The window looked sealed, but it was an old building. That might be a possibility. She could do the television move and throw a chair through it. At least she thought so. A building this old couldn't have bulletproof glass. Wait. Did she really just think about television at a time like this? Or about needing to escape from a police station? And about throwing a chair through a window? Well, it would certainly be a comedy at this point. She couldn't imagine being able to climb out that window if it did break. She chuckled inside at the thought of how that would play out, with her landing on her face in the parking lot and the headlines reading: Mother of two fails to escape from police station after claiming to be attacked by officer while at work. No wonder the officer didn't believe her. It did sound insane.

"Officer Yates," Kate started, "I know I must seem crazy to you. But I was going to lunch at work and some man grabbed my arm and slammed me against the car and told me he wanted a file that I don't have. I managed to escape, and when he raised his arms, I saw he had a gun and a badge."

"Well, Miss, I'm sure what happened to you was very scary. Are you hurt?"

"No, I'm just shaken up and not sure what to do or why he attacked me or what he wanted or --" Kate rambled on in rapid fire style.

"Ma'am. Ma'am. Slow down."

"But he was a cop!"

"Did he take anything from you or harm you in any way?"

"No, but –"

"Did anyone else see this?" the officer asked.

"I don't know. I don't think so."

"Are you having any problems with anyone at work?"

"No. And this man didn't work with me. He was a cop!'

"Ma'am. You really must stop saying that if you want our help; it's a very serious charge. Were you doing something illegal?"

46

"No!" Kate snapped. "I was walking to my car at work, and he just came out of nowhere. But I'm telling you he had a badge and a gun."

"Ma'am, if he had a badge and a gun, why would he need to attack you rather than just arrest you? Did you resist arrest?"

"No. I was – I-I was…" Kate stopped to think. Why *would* he attack me if he had a gun and a badge? A surge of cold overcame Kate. Something was not right here.

"Ma'am, do you want to start at the beginning, and I can put your statement on file?"

"On file?" Kate exclaimed angrily.

"Yes, that's the procedure. If you aren't hurt, and he didn't take anything, we'll leave the case open with our detectives until more evidence shows up."

On file wasn't going to help Kate solve this mystery, but she knew better than to not put something on paper with law enforcement in case anything else turned up. "Ok, let's get started," Kate agreed half-heartedly.

After a grueling 45 minutes with Officer Yates, Kate had put her story on paper. She was satisfied that at least it was recorded but knew that nothing else would be done to solve the crime. Was it a crime? Yes, that was assault. Or battery. She wasn't sure which was which, but it was one of them. Somehow reciting the story to someone who recorded it made it seem less scary, though.

"Ok, Ms. O'Connor, I think we have everything we need now. This sounds like a case of mistaken identity to me. I'm sure everything will be fine. Feel free to let us know if anything else happens."

Anything else? Like someone actually kidnapping me next time, Kate thought to herself. "Ok, thanks." Kate scanned the parking lot for the unmarked car that arrived with Officer Yates. It was gone. Kate took her keys out of her purse and slid them between her fingers, just in case. She walked swiftly to her car and got in. Maybe she was just paranoid, and it was mistake. Now what? Jason. She needed to talk to Jason. No, his conspiracy mindset would jump to the worst. He was at his new job. She didn't need him to get fired because his crazy wife showed up panicked one day with a tale about cops attacking her. It seemed the danger was over; Officer Yates was probably right. It probably was a case of mistaken identity.

Chapter 8

Kate started toward work and decided against it. She had a sick day coming. She just needed to let her boss know. She could handle that with an email once she got home. She didn't really think she should tell people at work about her experience. If no one saw it, they'd probably react the way Officer Yates did. It did sound far-fetched even to her. A man with a gun and a badge attacked her in a wide-open parking lot in the middle of the day, promising not to hurt her if she turned over a file? No witnesses, no bruises? Yeah, a hot shower and some yoga pants is what she needed. And maybe some ice cream.

The green veneer house was set back in the woods off the main road about 300 feet. Kate and Jason liked the feeling of being in the country in the middle of the city. They would live further out in the country if they could find jobs within driving range, but the job market in Atlanta was competitive and the traffic more than a bear. Each morning they went their separate ways, to opposite ends of metro Atlanta. Kate had the better drive, going north away from traffic to a small town, while Jason headed east, dead into the traffic each morning. He wouldn't be home for hours. The kids were at Grandma's until 6. Much needed solitude was awaiting Kate as she pulled into the garage. She closed the door so no one would know she was home yet.

Kate rolled her eyes as she passed through the kitchen. Why is my house always such a mess? She threw off her clothes and hopped into the shower. Tears welled up as she began to pray, "Lord, I'm not sure what happened today but thank you for getting me through it. Help Jason understand why I didn't come straight to him." She stood in the shower until the water ran cold, exited and put on her comfort clothes. As soon as she plopped on the bed for a nap she realized that she needed to email her boss about not coming back to work. How exactly was she going to explain this?

Kate wondered into the den to retrieve the ipad. She sat on the couch staring at the kids' clothes and toys on the floor. Wow. I really am letting the kids get out of control. Well, they can clean it up when they return, she thought.

She opened the ipad and started an email to Jim. She wrote 7 drafts before deciding on a simple sentence that didn't contain a lie. She sent it quickly before changing her mind again. She pondered sending one to her husband but decided to wait to tell him in person. No need to worry him now. As she went to close the ipad, she decided to check her personal email. Junk, junk, and more junk, she thought. Still, she clicked on the email from xdrenlaine.com. After all, she still wanted that coupon.

The email opened and read, "POMB #1257." How odd, she thought. What is POMB #1257?

Kate paced in the den, trying to answer questions in her mind. She didn't remember the house being that disheveled when she left. It wasn't a disaster area, but she was a neat freak, and there seemed to be more out of place than she would normally let slide. She went to her bedroom closet to get a blanket and noticed two of her dresser drawers were slightly open. Two she rarely gets anything out of. And then it dawned on her. Someone had been looking for something and was trying to cover it up. Kate checked under the bed. The fire box was still there. She wondered if it was empty as she grabbed the key. There wasn't much of value in the house, but she did have $4,000 stashed in the fire box. She opened it to find everything still in place. Ok, maybe she was just crazy. The incident in the parking lot and now a home invasion? Surely not in the same day. Kate went back to the bathroom and looked around. A blouse was on the floor in her closet. Her hair dryer was put up in its holder. Ok, that was odd. She didn't remember putting it back this morning. Jason's closet door was closed. All the way. The door stuck and didn't close well. Yeah, someone was here, she thought. What if they were still in the house? What if they were coming back? What were they after? Whoever had been looking for something wasn't interested in money or her things. The file! They were looking for the file, whatever that meant.

She stood in the kitchen with her hands on her hips, wondering what file they were looking for. Why would she have a file? Her mind went to the email. POMB #1257. That had to be the link. Maybe the file was at POMB #1257. But what was that? Kate racked her brain to think of possibilities. After about 20 seconds, she wondered if it stood for post office mail box? There was a post office about a mile from her house; could that be POMB? #1257 had to be a mail box, but how was she going to get into it, exactly? Why was that message sent? Was it meant for her? What was in the box? Why was a cop after it?

Kate went back to the lock box and grabbed the money along with the passports, just in case. Now she felt like she was in some sort of bad action film. Really? Passports? Where exactly do you think you are going? She thought. She rolled her eyes and continued, determined not to end up like all those dumb women in the lame television shows she watches. It seemed a little over the top, but someone was definitely after her, and she needed to find that file and get somewhere safe.

Kate grabbed Jason's go-bag out of the closet. She picked up the 30/30 rifle and what she thought was the ammunition. She wondered if she could load it and fire it if necessary. She didn't mind weapons, just didn't really know how to use them. And she really hated to admit even to herself that Jason's offer to teach her how to shoot would have been nice to have about right now. Just in case, she grabbed the sharpest knife she could find, some first aid supplies, all the bottled water in the pantry, some extra clothes for her and Jason, towels and granola bars. As she loaded the car, she decided to grab Jason's toolbox, tent and machete as well as the ipad. Maybe she wasn't a prepper like Jason's nerdy group, but she was a mom and new how to plan ahead. The kids! What was she going to do about the kids?

Kate quickly opened the ipad up again and emailed her mom. Fortunately, Grandma was with the times somewhat and could read email. "Have to do something at church and will be late tonight. Can you feed and keep kids until I return? Lost my phone somewhere; I'll call when I find it," she typed and sent.

Now for Jason. That's a little trickier. Well, he won't read it for a while anyway. "Hey. Lots of strange stuff going on. I need you to meet me at the church after work. Mom has kids. I lost my phone somewhere, so email is all I have for now."

Kate closed the ipad once again and headed to the car. She felt terrified and silly all at the same time. She was a normal person, wasn't she? Do normal people pack rifles and knives in their car to drive to the post office and investigate a mystery file on a hunch that someone had searched their house? Could she even take a firearm into the parking lot at a post office? Kate covered the rifle, just in case. Confident she was overprepared for something, she headed toward the post office. Her mind raced with more questions. What was in the box? And how was she going to get into it?

Why was the email sent to her? Was she the intended recipient? Who was that man at the school? Why was a cop interested in the file? What was on the file? Who was in her house? What exactly was her plan? For the first time in a long time, she had no idea.

Chapter 9

Kate pulled into the parking lot next to the post office just in case there was a rule about rifles. She was still unsure of her plan as she entered the post office and searched for #1257. The numbers ended at 1101. There was not a box with #1257. That would have been too easy anyway, she thought. "POMB, POMB," she muttered under her breath as she walked back to the car, racking her brain for another solution. She was acting insane. This had to be a case of mistaken identity. But they were in her house! Right? Or did she imagine that? She started to doubt anything that happened today. She drove aimlessly in the city, trying to decide if POMB meant anything or if she was just overreacting.

Occasionally, Kate circled back or made an odd turn, to see if anyone was following her. She was fortunate to live in a heavily populated suburb in which two-lane roads were most common. If someone was following her, it would be difficult for them to get too close without her noticing. She drove around a few parking lots, hoping to get any ideas to help her solve the mystery.

As she pulled out of the WalMart lot, Kate looked in the rear-view mirror and saw a green Toyota creeping toward her. She thought she might have seen it a few minutes earlier on Mitchell Road when she turned into the Kohl's lot. Was someone following her? Or was that paranoia? Kate exited the lot and pushed the pedal hard. She got up to speed quickly and made the next right. Fortunately, it was a winding road with curves that came quickly. She couldn't see if the car was still there. She pressed on, making the next two lefts and then an immediate right. She spotted a car wash on the right and pulled in nearly on two wheels. She frantically feed the machine to open the bars for the car wash, constantly checking in her mirror. She didn't see the green car. Was she losing her, mind or had she actually lost a tail? She wasn't sure. She sat in silence as the wash engulfed her car. Her heart was racing thinking about what to do next. She was a good driver, but she certainly was not skilled enough to lose a professional tail without crashing. She hoped she was wrong about the green Toyota. As the car wash finished up she took a deep breath, hoping no one was on the other side waiting for her. Kate slowly eased the car out of the wash tunnel, carefully checking for a green Toyota. None in sight.

Relieved, Kate realized she wasn't exactly sure where she was. She had grown up in this area, but it was so much more developed than when she was a child. She rolled down her window and asked the attendant, "Excuse me, can you tell me if we are close to 92 here?"

The chunky teen slung his long hair out of his eyes and leaned down to her window. "It's just up ahead at the next light next to Burger King. Can't miss it."

"Thank you," Kate said as she rolled up the window and checked the rear view again. No sign of her tail. She headed for 92 and decided to proceed to the church.

Chapter 10

At 5:12, Kate pulled into the church parking lot. She wasn't surprised to see other cars, as one of the things she loved most about her church is that the building was open to the community most nights. Her church family believed in being part of the community and put their money where their mouth was. They let local schools, the fire department and local law enforcement all use the building for any number of events. There were more cars than she anticipated, though, for a Friday night. She didn't want to park too far out that Jason would miss her car, but she needed to stay where he could easily spot her car and park next to her. It would be a risk having to go into the church to find him if all this was real. And she didn't know who was after her or even if anyone was. She realized should have said, "parking lot" in her email. Watching and criticizing cloak and dagger stories was clearly different than being in one, she thought. Kate scanned the lot and chose a spot just to the right of the new children's building where they often parked on Sunday mornings. She waited patiently, watching for Jason's car, thinking he'd be a creature of habit and park on that side of the building.

A large blue van pulled into the spot next to her, blocking her view of the lot entrance. Kate would have to move. She cranked the car and started to back out when someone tapped on her driver's side window. Startled, Kate turned to see her friend Melissa with a big goofy grin on her face. Kate stopped the car and rolled the window down.

"Hey, friend! What are you doing here?"

Kate thought quickly on her feet, careful not to stray too far from the truth, as she was a terrible liar. "Just meeting up with my husband."

"Got a hot date planned?" Melissa joked.

"Something like that."

"I'm jealous. Brian is working so much these days. I can't remember the last time we got out. Hey, look at this new purse I got from my friend Shelly – she sells that ThirtyOne stuff." Melissa pushed the bag inside the car window expecting Kate to inspect it. "It has like six different pockets. Pretty cool, huh?"

"Yeah, I really like that for you. It suits you." Kate responded hastily, trying to balance her friendship with her need to find Jason before he entered the church.

"Listen, I'm late, but I'll call you later, ok?" Melissa must have sensed Kate's disinterest.

"Ok." Kate was glad that her friend was in a hurry. She needed to move her car and get in position for Jason to see her car. Kate put the car in reverse and started to back out of the spot just in time to see Jason enter the building. So much for that plan.

Kate slammed the car back in part, grabbed the backpack and hurriedly entered the church. The main entrance was open and welcoming, leading to a large foyer area with a two-story glass ceiling, branded signage to direct visitors, a kiosk staffed with church workers most nights, and a coffee bar. It was a big church, but one where Kate and Jason felt comfortable. Jason stepped toward the doors and greeted her with a kiss on the cheek. "There's my lovely wife," he said affectionately.

Kate loved that Jason always took the time to give her a compliment, but in this case, she needed to speed things along. She quickly leaned in to kiss him back on the cheek, grabbed his hand and pulled toward the exit. "Come on, we have to go," she whispered in his ear.

"Go where?" Jason asked, planting his feet.

"Just come on, ok?" Kate started walking, pulling Jason's hand.

Jason complied but thought the behavior was odd, even for his wife. "What was up with that cryptic email and wanting to meet me here?" There was no answer. Jason noticed the bag on Kate's shoulder. "And why do you have my go-bag?"

"Look, it's a long story, and we need to get moving. Do you trust me?"

"You know I do, but I'd like to know where we are going."

Kate dropped Jason's hand and walked quickly out of the main pathway for visitors arriving and leaned toward the wall. She motioned for Jason to come toward her, and he complied. Kate usually enjoyed his relaxed state and poked fun at his saunter, but she needed him to kick it up a notch. "Someone grabbed me work today," she started.

"I want to grab you right here, but we are in church." Jason joked. Kate usually enjoyed her husband's humor and playful manner, but not now. She needed him to focus.

"Listen," Kate scolded. "I'm serious."

Jason immediately had regret for making a joke. "What happened?"

"Some guy with a badge and a gun grabbed me in the parking lot at work. He wanted some file."

"What? Kate, what are you talking about? Are you ok?" Jason scanned his wife for bruises, grabbing her arms to investigate further.

"Yeah, I'm fine --" Kate answered, dismissing Jason's concern and pushing his hands away.

"Did you call the police?"

"He was the police – or at least I think he might have been," Kate answered.

"What? That's insane! Why would a cop attack you? "

"I'm not sure, but I think –" Kate stopped talking. She spotted a man who looked very much like her attacker entering the church.

"Kate? Kate? Earth to Kate?"

Kate pushed her hands to Jason's mouth to stop him from talking. Her eyes fixated on a man walking toward the stairs. She backed into the hallway a little more and peered around the corner.

Jason stepped in front of her to get her attention. "What are you doing?" Jason asked, unamused at her.

"Shhh!" She commanded, pushing Jason aside to get a better look. He was certainly the right build from the man she encountered earlier today. Different clothes, though. He was wearing a suit with a white Chaps button-down shirt, and solid black tie. His brown hair was cut high and tight, like a Marine. That part she remembered clearly from the encounter.

 "Kate – "

"Shhh! Wait a minute," Kate whispered, pointing her finger at him like a child. She stared at the man as he turned toward the stairs. His face angled just enough for Kate to confirm it was him. What was he doing here? Kate watched him start up the stairs and noticed that he had a gun holstered on his hip. He wasn't dressed in a uniform, though. Who brings a weapon to church? Kate almost chuckled inside as she remembered that she had Jason's 30/30 in her car, but she was too scared to laugh. This was her attacker, walking around like nothing was going on. Was he a cop? And more importantly, did he know she was there? Kate watched him enter room 222.

"Kate – what's going on?" Jason asked again, clearly frustrated with her at this point.

Ignoring her husband, Kate scanned the lobby again trying to decide what to do next. Her attacker was upstairs, and he had a gun. She grabbed Jason's hand and pulled him reluctantly to the marquee sign in the lobby. It read:

> North Paulding Band Concert   RM 201
>
> FBI Award Ceremony   RM 222

Her attacker was an FBI agent?

"I just saw the guy that attacked me in the parking lot at work. Look! He's an FBI agent!"

"Kate, this is nuts. An FBI agent? Really? What has gotten into you?"

"I'm being serious. I left for lunch at work today and some guy – that FBI agent I just saw – grabbed me in the parking lot. He wanted me to give him the file. I have no idea what file he wanted. He said he wouldn't hurt me if I would give it to him. I managed to push him down and get away."

"Wait. Some guy grabbed you in the parking lot at work? During the day?"

"Yes, that's what I've been trying to tell you."

Still having trouble processing it, Jason asked, "And YOU were able to get away?"

"Yeah, I pushed him down."

"You pushed him down?" Jason repeated in disbelief.

"Yeah, I did," Kate said, proud of herself.

"And nobody came to help you? Why didn't you call me, Kate?" Jason asked angrily, clearly wanting to protect his wife.

"I couldn't find my phone. I still can't."

"And did anyone call the police?"

"Well, I didn't tell anyone. I was afraid they wouldn't believe me. So, I went to the police station, but they couldn't help me. I just can't figure out why an FBI agent thinks I have a file."

"Are you sure that was the man who attacked you? It's hard to believe an FBI agent did that, Kate. I'm so glad you weren't hurt, but perhaps you are mistaken. You have to admit; it's a little strange to think an FBI agent attacked you in broad daylight for no reason, and you were able to get away."

"No, that's him. I'm sure of it."

"Ok, Ok, but why? And why not just show you his badge?" Jason asked, still skeptical of Kate's story.

Kate was a little frustrated with Jason's disbelief of her story, but she understood his hesitancy. She knew he was truly trying to help, and besides, she had the exact same questions.

Sirens sounded outside the church. While not an unusual sound, this was much louder than one or two. Kate ran toward the front door to see 7 or 8 cop cars arriving in the parking lot blocking the exit. Could this be another coincidence? Probably not. Kate walked over to the reception desk and asked the church worker what was going on. She was on the phone and held her hand out with her finger up to indicate she was busy listening. After a couple of minutes, she hung up the phone.

Kate repeated her question and the receptionist whispered, "The cops said someone gave them a tip about a possible vehicle involved in the death of that man found in Seven Hills."

Death of a man in Seven Hills? That was right behind the kids' school! What man?

"Give me your phone," Kate instructed Jason.

Kate didn't wait for Jason's slow reach to pull the phone all the way out of his pocket. She reached for it and knocked it out of his hands. The phone crashed to the floor. Kate and Jason knocked heads as they bent to get it. Kate got to it first and stood up, trying desperately to Google 'man found dead in Seven Hills'.

"Come on!" Kate yelled at the phone as it churned trying to load search selections.

"Patience, Grasshopper," Jason said with a smile.

"Here it is," Kate said, sharing the phone view with Jason. "Police on high alert after man found stabbed to death in Seven Hills." Kate clicked for more information. The phone once again hesitated, and Kate stomped her foot like a child. "Come on!"

Finally, the page loaded, and Kate read out loud quicker than Jason could follow, "A local community is rocked by the death of a man in their quiet suburban neighborhood. Forty-six-year-old Scott Brown was found dead stabbed to death in Seven Hills. A woman jogging found his body around 5am Friday just outside the neighborhood pool. No witnesses have come forward, and police are searching for any clues. Scott Brown was an employee of US Investigations Services. He was unmarried and lived in Virginia Beach. It is unknown why Brown was in the area. If you have any details, please call Crime Stoppers at 800-555-9292. Check back for updates as more details become available." Kate scrolled further. Nausea and pain overcame her as she saw the picture of the victim. It was the man in the white Honda. Panic set it. Kate wasn't sure what to do.

"What is your deal, Kate?" Jason asked, still unsure what was going on with his wife.

"I have a lot more to tell you, but we need to get out of here first and go somewhere more secluded to figure this out."

"Well, apparently, cops are blocking the exit." Jason reminded Kate.

"Yeah. That's a problem."

"Look, I'm not sure what all is going on here, but let's take a minute and think. Let's go to the police and talk to them. They are already here for some other reason anyway." Jason offered.

"No, we have to get out of here!" Kate insisted.

"Kate, we can't leave. The police are here."

Kate leaned in to whisper in Jason's ear. "The dead guy is the guy from the school parking lot!"

Jason didn't panic. "Ok, let's just tell the police your story. I'm sure we can sort this out."

Kate pulled Jason out of earshot of anyone around. In the confusion, most people were staring out the window and asking questions of the church personnel, not paying attention to Kate and Jason, but she didn't want to take any chances. Kate said softly but sternly, "I did already, and they didn't help me. The man who was killed gave me that coupon to Xdrenaline yesterday in the school parking lot. The guy who attacked me is an

FBI agent, and he's upstairs. I have your 30/30 and a bunch of prepper stuff in my car. They are looking for a suspect. And if I were the police, I'd look pretty guilty about right now."

"What? You have the 30/30 in the car? Ok, Kate, let's go talk to the police or the FBI agent you think attacked you."

"Are you listening to me? I have a weapon in the car. At church. Where they are searching for a killer. And the FBI attacked me."

Jason wanted to question her further, but he sensed the seriousness in her voice. He had never seen her this way and knew he would rather be safe than sorry when it came to protecting his family.

"Can you call your MAG group? It's not the apocalypse, but it's an emergency. And trust me on this – I need them to go to the house and protect our family," Kate said hastily.

Jason knew if she was asking for help from his MAG group, she was serious. From that point on, he stopped trying to figure Kate out and started formulating a plan. Jason took the phone from Kate and dialed his friend Norman. Kate listened to Jason's side of the conversation, anxious about how they were going to get out.

"Hey, I need some help. There is something major going on at our church, and we need to leave. How quickly can you pick us up on the south side of Due West?"

Jason paused for the answer. "Ok, I need to enact emergency plan F and send the rest of the team to our house and set up camp. They need to protect the kids and my in-laws. I'll fill you in when we see you. South side of Due West. 5 minutes."

The police hadn't set up a perimeter yet, so whatever they were doing wasn't a manhunt. Still, Jason knew the best time to leave was now before that started. There was a clear path to Due West, but it was in the open. Instead, they would need to trek through the pond on the back side of the church and through the woods to remain unseen. And they needed to hurry. It was only about 100 yards, but Jason wondered if Kate's knee could hold out, and if she could move fast enough to not been seen. At least she had on dark colored clothes. Jason started trying to think of a story in case they were caught by the police. Nothing came to mind.

"Give me the pack, and follow me," Jason ordered.

Kate handed the pack over and followed Jason through the church halls. They were swimming upstream in the crowd, as people were starting to gather in the lobby to watch the police. Kate gripped Jason's hand tight to not lose him, and they made it to the back hall quickly. Jason turned right to head for an exit.

"No, that one locks you in the playground," Kate whispered. "This way," she instructed.

Jason changed directions and stopped just short of the door. He needed to get a good look at what was going on before exiting the building. The last thing he wanted to do was run into a cop on the backside of the building and have to explain the contents of Kate's car.

"If they stop us, we were going for ice cream since we couldn't leave in the car, ok?" Jason said.

Kind of thin, but at least it's something, Kate thought. "Got it. "

It appeared all clear. Jason pulled Kate's hand as they exited the building and started for the pond. Kate was trying to keep up, ignoring the pain in her knee with every step. It had been a long time since she ran anywhere. Every joint ached as they trotted to the pond. They reached the pond, and Jason entered first, carefully not to make a lot of splash. There had been a drought, and the pond was less than knee deep. Kate followed Jason into the pond hesitantly. She hated creepy crawlies and thought of ponds and lakes as dirty bath water with monsters in them. She liked to look at them or ride on top, but she wasn't too fond of being in them. Fortunately, it was only about 40 steps across, but it was like walking in sand, each step putting pressure on Kate's knee. She held her breath as they crossed and tried not to think about what else was in the pond with her. The water was cold and sent pain up her body like shards of glass. As they approached the edge, Jason climbed out first. He knew Kate would have trouble getting out. He sat on the bank, planted his feet in the soft ground, and reached for Kate's hand. Suddenly he heard the cops in the distance. He looked up to see two uniformed officers moving that direction. They would have to move faster.

"Kate, we have to move," Jason whispered.

"I know, I know," Kate answered softly. She grabbed his hand, pulled hard and tried to scale the small hill. Her foot slipped, knocking her down onto her knees splashing slightly. She and Jason froze, hoping the sound didn't travel. Her face was only inches from the dirty cold water. She hesitated while they waited to see if there was any movement near them. Jason motioned for her to move, and she grabbed his foot and pulled hard, scaling the hill and falling face first on top of him. It wasn't graceful, but at least she made it. Jason snickered silently at the fall and wanted to kiss his wife, but he knew they needed to move. Kate scrambled to her feet and ran as fast as she could through the woods with Jason following. They cleared the trees and walked toward the road.

Jason was happy to see Norman's Jeep pull into the intersection just as they approached.

"This is just like Budapest all over again," Kate said through heaving breaths, making her reference to *The Avengers*.

"You and I remember Budapest very differently," Jason responded. He and Kate quoted movies and television shows to each other frequently.

Jason waved at Norman and approached the Jeep that had stopped at the light. He pushed Kate from the backside into the Jeep and hopped into the passenger seat. "Where to?" Norman asked.

"Home, I guess," Jason said.

"No, we can't go there. Someone broke in earlier," Kate shouted.

"What? I thought you said someone attacked you at work" Jason argued.

"I did. That FBI agent. But someone also broke into the house," Kate said, exacerbated. "We have to get out of town. They were looking for a file."

"Wait. An FBI agent attacked you and broke into your house?" Norman asked.

"Yes. Well, I think. I don't know. I just know we have to get somewhere safe until I figure it out," Kate answered.

"How about Mike's place in Pine Mountain?" Norman offered.

"Think he'll mind?" Jason asked.

"Nah, he's home for two more weeks," Norman said. "I talked to him yesterday. I can call him on the way for a heads-up."

"Ok, then let's go there," Jason said.

"You got it, brother," Norman said as he started down the road. The Jeep wasn't fancy and looked like Norman used it more off road than on. He reeked of ex-military with his short brown hair, camouflage fatigues and combat boots. He was definitely not someone you wanted to mess with in an ally, or anywhere, though Kate would bet he had seen his share of fights and won most of them. There was a dip cup between his legs and a weapon on his hip. She couldn't help but notice the worn-out version of the Bible on his back seat. She picked it up and squeezed it to her chest, hoping just being near God's word would protect her. She closed her eyes and let tears roll down as she thanked God for Norman and this dorky MAG group her husband had found.

"Ick," Kate announced. She was wet and dirty from the pond. Her feet were cold and wet. Kate took her shoes and socks off and handed them up front to Jason. "Will you put these in front of the heat coming out up there?" she asked.

Jason took the shoes and did as she asked. "Are you cold?"

"There are blankets behind you and some hand warmers in the brown bag. Get what you need," Norman offered.

"Thanks," Kate responded as she climbed halfway over the seat to see the blanket and bag. She pulled blanket over her and handed one of the hand warmers to Jason. "Will you open this for me?"

Jason opened the hand warmer packet and gave it back to Kate. She had to reposition in order to fold her feet one at a time in the bend of her knee to get her toes warm. She used the warmer for her hands.

"Jason – will you call my mom? Tell her as little as possible about what is actually going on."

"Well," Jason said, "That should be easy since I don't know what is going on."

Kate gave him snarky face. "I'll explain it all in a minute. Just tell her I forgot your MAG group is doing an exercise this weekend and ask if she'll keep the kids until we get back. Let her know part of the exercise is the MAG group will be patrolling our house so she won't worry when she sees them at the house. Tell her I'll call her when I find my phone but that I'm busy right now."

Jason said, "That's a lot to remember. Why don't you just call her yourself?"

"Because you know I don't lie well. She'll know something is up," Kate protested.

"And I lie well?" Jason asked, offended.

"No, but you are so even keel. She won't hear trouble in your voice. Please, Jason."

Jason knew she was right and made the call. He forgot to tell Kate's mom about the MAG group and had to make a second call.

Kate's mind raced with all that had happened in the last 24 hours. Did she and Jason really just escape from the police? Was an FBI agent after her? This was stuff that her crazy television shows were made of. It couldn't be real. Could it?

After Jason finished the calls, he turned to Kate. "We have 2 hours before we get to Mike's. Start from the beginning this time and tell me everything."

Chapter 11

It was dark when they arrived at Mike's house, which sat back on 50 acres of rolling pastures and thickets of pine trees. Her shoes were still damp, but her clothes had dried out. Mike's place had two different ponds, one clearly used for fishing and one for swimming, complete with a dock, pedal boats, and a canoe. A chicken coup was to the left of the backyard, and Kate could see shadows of horses and cows in one of the adjacent fields under the moonlight. His driveway was a mixture of sand, rock and mud along with a lot of holes, something the Jeep had no problem navigating. As they pulled toward the house, Mike greeted them from the porch.

"Hey, folks! It's not much, but you're welcome to come in stay as long as you need," Mike said with the charm of a true Southerner.

"Thanks, Mike," Jason said with a smile. They shook hands, and Kate realized how much taller Mike was than her husband. Mike had been the leader of the MAG group before moving south of Atlanta last year. It had been a while since Jason had spoken of him, and Kate had never met him. Mike was also military. If it weren't for the accent, Kate thought he could probably double for Stone Cold Steve Austin, not that Kate would ever be caught watching WWE trash. "This is my wife, Kate."

"Pleased to meet you," Mike said, removing his hat and bowing his head slightly.

"And you as well. Thank you for letting us stay," Kate answered, offering her hand for a shake. Mike obliged. The two locked hands; Kate anticipated a firm grip, so she grabbed hard. As expected, the handshake was quick and powerful. A little too powerful for her taste.

"Happy to oblige. From what Norman told me, you have had quite a day, little lady," Mike said.

Kate smiled. Little lady. She hadn't heard that in a while. Jason had a strong Mississippi accent and loved to use old Southern phrases, but it had been a while since anyone had used that term referring to her. Kate certainly was not little, but she liked to think of herself as a lady when it was convenient. She took an instant liking to Mike for that phrase. "Yeah, I'm not entirely sure I understand what is going on."

"Well, that makes two of us. Let's go in and maybe we can help you sort it out," Mike offered with his hand pointing toward the door like Vanna White. Kate grabbed the backpack she had packed from the house and started to follow the others inside. "Here, let me get that for you," Mike offered, taking the backpack from her and holding the door open.

The house was built in the late 80s. The outside was cedar panels, and the inside boasted vaulted popcorn ceilings and hardwood floors. Mike's taste in décor was virtually nonexistent. The house was sparse, but clean and orderly. There were not any pictures hung on the walls but a couple of standing photos in frames on the top of the television cabinet. Kate couldn't see the details from where she stood and didn't want to appear nosey, but she glanced at the photos long enough to see one that must be of Mike and his unit. They were dressed in military fatigues in front of a green building. Another looked like a wedding picture from Mike's younger days. A third had a boy swinging on a playground. Kate sat on what she thought might be an uncomfortable leather couch but was surprised by its soft feel and cushy seat. She leaned back and rested her head on the back and drew the backpack up to her lap. She began to rifle through it, not sure exactly what she had managed to cram inside the pack versus what she had to leave in the car. She pulled out the ipad and charger, a change of clothes for her and Jason, his machete, and the travel wallet with cash and passports. The outside front pocket was filled with Band-Aids, gauze, and some sort of antibiotic cream. She was pleased with her stash, but her stomach rumbled as she realized she hadn't eaten since early this morning.

"Jason, you and Kate can stay in the spare bedroom to the left of the den. I'm in the master just next door. Norman and I will take shifts tonight on over watch. Help yourself to anything you need. There is some left over pizza in the fridge and cokes in the garage if you are hungry. After you get settled, we'll go through a debrief and get a plan together. For now, let's stay off all communication channels."

Kate stood from the couch slowly, her knee throbbing from all the activity today. She stumbled slightly as she started to walk, her ankles popping with every step. She wondered down the hall to the restroom and went in. Kate looked at the small shower, thankful that at least it was indoors and probably hot. She'd tackle that after getting something to eat.

Kate walked to the kitchen to find Jason had set the table with pizza and coke. The pizza had been a supreme, but Jason had gone to the trouble to take off the many of the toppings for Kate to make it to her liking. She appreciated his thoughtfulness but was embarrassed by everyone knowing how picky she was. After all, these guys were used to the harshest conditions in the military. She must look like a spoiled princess to them. Instead of jeers and condescension she anticipated from Mike and Norman, she got nothing but smiles. She sat down and began to eat, grateful for her husband and his friends.

"Kate, do you really think it was an FBI agent that grabbed you in the parking lot at work?" Norman asked.

"Yeah, I could be wrong, but I'm sure he had a badge and a gun. I'm pretty sure we saw him at the church going to an FBI event."

"Well, we'll try to sort this out after dinner," Mike said. He had a comforting presence, much like Jason. She felt safe with Jason and his friends. "Let's say grace."

Kate was surprised at the gesture, but more surprised at the sincere prayer that Mike offered in front of her and Jason. It wasn't fluffy or a surface prayer. Mike took the opportunity to really speak his heart to God. He offered praise and thanksgiving for individual blessings God had provided followed by a sincere asking of wisdom to provide safety to the four of them while sorting the situation out. He even confessed a specific sin he was struggling to overcome. She had an entirely different vision of these guys. She knew that Mike had often talked about building the group on Christian principles, but she wasn't sure exactly what that meant. The sincerity of his prayer almost brought Kate to tears.

There wasn't much small talk after the prayer. The four of them ate the left-over pizza almost in silence. After dinner, Kate felt compelled to clear the table and clean up, and then the four of them went to Mike's "command center" in the basement. They entered a downstairs den, and Mike pushed on what looked to be an ordinary wood panel to reveal an opening to a hidden room with reinforced concrete. Kate was a bit uneasy about all the weapons hanging on the wall in the room but took comfort in how neat and organized they were, and the fact that these guys knew how to use the weapons. She counted 8 monitors in the room and a lot of equipment she wasn't sure what it was.

"What is all this, Mike?" Kate asked curiously.

"Security measures. Things tend to follow you when you are on a kill squad in the middle of a war, so I am prepared. Makes over watch pretty simple, actually. Not many people are going to get by this stuff without me knowing."

For a moment, she felt like she was in a James Bond movie. The she remembered this was real and fear overcame her once again.

"Ok, let's get started. Kate, I need you to sign into your email account so we can look at that communication."

"I thought we were staying off communication channels. What if they track it somehow?" Kate questioned.

"We don't know who 'they' is. Unless you want to trust the police or your new FBI friend, we have to solve this somehow, and that means starting at the beginning," Mike replied.

Kate looked at Jason for guidance. "Go ahead. He's right."

Kate sat in the worn office chair and logged into her email on Mike's computer. There were 20 new emails, one of which was from Xdrenlaine. She froze. The subject line read: The deal you've been waiting for is heer. More misspellings. And this one had an attachment on it. She looked back at Jason. "There's a new one. Which one do you want to see first?"

"Let's start with the first one," Jason replied.

Kate opened the first one and showed it to Mike and Norman. "POMB #1257," read Mike. "Ok, that's some sort of code or location we have to figure out."

Then she clicked the new email. "Now open Sundays," it read. There was an attachment. Kate clicked hesitantly, not sure what would happen. An Excel file downloaded onto Mike's computer. Mike sprang into action and quickly cut the connection in case there was a tracker in the download. He hoped he had stopped anyone from finding them. No one in the room was sure how all that geek stuff worked, but they all imagined like in the movies that some hacker somewhere could figure out what they were doing and trace it back to Mike's IP address to get a location. All of this seemed surreal to Kate, but she'd rather be safe than sorry.

"Ok, we are offline. Jason, you are the Excel expert. You're up." Mike ordered.

Jason moved to the computer and switched places with Kate. He opened the Excel file. It was thousands of lines of numbers. He scrolled to the right to find it ended at column AB. There were no headers, nothing to make sense out of at first glance. The four of them stared at the spreadsheet clueless as to what they had.

Finally, Kate blurted out the obvious in exasperation, "This is the file the FBI agent wanted. Scott Brown was killed before passing it to me. Now we are all in danger!"

Mike was quick and measured in his response, "Kate, don't panic. It's important that we stay calm and think through this together."

Kate screamed, animated with her hand gestures and tears streaming down her face, "Don't panic? Don't panic? A man who passed me a flyer containing some super-secret file in my kids' school parking lot is now dead, the police think I am the crazed killer on the loose, a rogue FBI agent attacked me in broad daylight in my work parking lot, someone broke into our house in the middle of the day, and we have no idea if someone is tracking our every move to kill us over a file we don't even know what it is! I think I'm way beyond panicking!"

Jason stood and grabbed his wife gently by the shoulders as she broke down. "We are going to figure this out, Kate."

She cried on his shoulder and whined through the tears, "I am a wife and a mother. I work in marketing. This doesn't make any sense!"

Jason joked by quoting Hawkeye from *Avengers: Age of Ultron*, "The city is flying! We're fighting an army of robots! And I have a bow and arrow! None of this makes sense!"

Jason's joke broke the tension. Kate laughed through her tears and said, "Why is this happening?"

"I don't know, Kate, but you know who does," Jason comforted.

"Yeah, I know. Do you think this counts as grumbling and complaining? My devotion yesterday was to do everything without grumbling and complaining."

"Yeah, I think you are going to have to work on that a little more," Jason said with a smile.

Kate laughed though the tears once more and then backed off Jason's shoulders. She wiped her tears and got her bearings. "Mike, do you have any markers for this white board?" Kate asked.

"Sure – top drawer on the left," Mike replied.

Kate pulled out the markers and started writing on the board. She figured if it works for *Castle* maybe it might work for her. Everything else about today seemed as unbelievable as the cop shows she enjoyed on television, and at this point, she didn't have much to lose.

Kate wrote "Victim: Scott Brown" on one side and "Attacker: FBI agent" on the other. Down below she wrote, "Motive: file." "Ok, what do we know about our victim?" Kate began talking as she was writing, "46, lives – um, lived – in Virginia, worked for US Investigations Services, found dead in Seven Hills, visited Frey Elementary, drove white Honda, computer savvy or knows someone who is, but not so savvy that they know how to encrypt files, and, he can't spell."

Norman spoke up and chuckled, "Hey, don't speak ill of the dead."

"It's a clue, isn't it?" Kate returned.

"Kate's right you guys," Jason stepped in. "And it wasn't just once he misspelled something."

"Yeah, at first, I thought it was a typo in the web address on the flyer, but that led us to an alternate website which also had multiple places where easy words had letters reversed. The second email contained letters reversed in the subject line." Kate asked.

"Kate, didn't you work as an investigator before we met?" Jason asked.

"Yeah, like 12 years ago," Kate answered.

"You were an investigator?" Norman asked in disbelief.

"Yeah, a special investigator with a top-secret clearance," Kate bragged. "I worked for the same company. We did security clearances and so forth. I wanted to fulfill that childhood dream of being a Charlie's Angel I guess," Kate said sarcastically. She held her fingers up and struck a Charlie's Angels' pose to make her point. And then she realized not only how silly she looked but how ridiculous it would have been for her to be a real detective or spy. She dropped her hands and her voice changed inflection, showing her self-doubt and disappointment. "But it was more of a red tape job than anything. We didn't do anything dangerous."

"Ok that's the link, though. Did you know Scott Brown?" Mike asked.

"No. Do you really think Scott Brown sought me out to give me that file? I kind of thought it was random."

"Maybe, but we can't rule it out at this point. The fact that he was in your neighborhood so far from his work and home and worked where you used to is too much of a coincidence," Mike answered.

"Ok, let's move to the FBI guy," Jason said.

"But I don't know anything about him." Kate said defeated.

"Sure you do," Jason challenged her, "he didn't reveal himself as law enforcement when he approached you."

"Yeah, that has to mean something – like he's involved in something under the table about this file. He also didn't want to hurt me or he would have. And he must work or live close to the area, as he was at the FBI award ceremony at our church tonight," Kate answered.

"Or he is in from out of town for some reason related or unrelated to our case," Jason challenged her again.

"Fine. You are right. He could live or work anywhere, just like our victim. It's possible they know each other. Maybe our FBI agent works or lives in Virginia," Kate posed.

"Perhaps," Jason replied. "Ok, so the file. We have this Excel file that we know is worth killing for. I'm going to have to study it before I have any ideas on what type of data they are trying to store."

"Ok, let's all try to get some rest for tonight. Norman and I have the over watch. We'll reconvene at 0700," Mike said.

"That's it? You guys are just going to quit?" Kate asked, astounded at the thought.

"Calm down, Kate. Everyone's brain doesn't work on overtime like yours," Jason said. "Why don't you take a shower while I work on this file."

Kate agreed and headed upstairs. She was tired and desperately wanted a shower. She gathered her things and went to the bathroom. She turned the water on and waited for it to get hot. Climbing in she noticed there was only bar soap available and no shampoo. Since Mike was bald, he didn't need shampoo. Kate hated the way bar soap felt on her skin, so she decided against washing her hair with it for now. She might have to settle for that tomorrow, but she knew if she used it, she wouldn't be able to comb through her hair. Suddenly she realized she hadn't gotten a towel out. She climbed back out of the shower and found 2 red towels in the cabinet next to some shampoo and conditioner. It looked old and nearly gone, but she hoped to get a few drops of each out. She worked the bottles and was successful. Staying in the shower until the water ran cold was her preference, but there were others in the house. She settled for turning her skin red and got out so someone else could have a turn. She wrapped one red towel around her head and another around her body. The one around her body didn't quite close all the way, but beggars couldn't be choosers. Red was an odd choice for towels she thought, but there wasn't much about this place that wasn't a little odd.

Kate looked into the fogged-up mirror and wondered how all this had happened. She was a normal, boring person with a family. And now she was caught up in some crazy action thriller she often watched on television. She dried off and put the change of clothes she brought on, the legs of the pants sticking to her wet body. She was sweating, something she had always seen as a sign of a good shower. Kate exited the bathroom and headed for the guest room. She collapsed on the bed and stared at the ceiling fan slowly turning above her to circulate heat, her mind working hard to solve the mystery of what had happened. Her eyes closed, and her brain stopped thinking.

A soft kiss woke Kate from a hard nap. Jason was leaning over her on the bed. "Nice nap, gorgeous?" Kate appreciated how calm he was, remembering small details about how to make her feel in the middle of this crisis.

"No, not really. What did you figure out?"

"Not a lot. I've sliced that data every way I can think of so far. It's just a bunch of numbers. There are four-digit numbers that repeat, six-digit numbers that repeat, eleven-digit numbers that repeat. There are time stamps that are unique and one column of 18 digits that are unique. There are dollar amounts in there, too. The data looks clean, meaning the columns are all the same input, but I'm not sure what any of them mean, though.

I figure it has to be tied to Scott's work somehow, and you are going to be the one to best decipher that."

Kate sighed. "Ok," she groaned as she started to get up.

Jason kissed her again and pushed her back on the bed. "Not now; it will keep. This is the first night we've had without the kids in nearly a year. Let's enjoy that."

"Really? Are you not the least bit concerned about what is going on?" Kate huffed.

"Concerned? Sure. Worried? No. I know who is in control, and I'm settled with that."

"Really? It's that easy for you?" Kate protested.

"Yep."

"You really think the kids are ok?"

"Oh yeah, Brett checked in a few minutes ago. No activity. Put it in God's hands and let it go, Kate." Jason was Kate's counter balance, and a good spiritual leader. He was right, and she knew it.

Chapter 12

Kate tossed and turned in the dark. The bed was hard, and the pillow was soft. Not a good combination for Kate. Her back started to get stiff. But the physical ailments weren't her only problem. She couldn't stop thinking about what had happened. Why did Scott Brown give her that file? What did the file mean? Kate tried counting sheep to stop her mind from focusing on it, but she wasn't successful, as the sheep started doing gymnastics over the fence in her mind. She flipped over and flopped until about 3 am. Finally, her tired body overtook her brain, and she fell asleep.

"Hey, Kate, let's go," Jason said softly.

The sun peered into the room, making Kate slow to open her eyes. She grumbled out loud, rolled to the outside of the bed and fought her way to her feet. "Wow, I'm old," she said as every joint popped.

"Mike has some eggs and waffles ready in the kitchen," Jason said.

"Hooray! No grumbling or complaining from me on that," Kate quipped with a smile as she walked to the kitchen. Jason enjoyed her lame humor and watching her enjoy herself. She was an interesting woman. Jason never had to ask her twice to do anything. He learned early in his marriage to Kate that he needed to be careful with phrases like, "I need to," because Kate would just do it for him. He liked that about her. As an analytical person sometimes stuck in analysis paralysis, he liked being paired with an opposite who could get things done. Kate was a woman of action and achievement, but she had a flare for melodrama and creativity. She worked hard, played hard, and unfortunately, cried hard. She was a perfectionist who constantly beat herself up about her work and her parenting skills, among other things. But when she was in her element, there was no one more fascinating to watch.

"Mmmmm, these are great, Mike," Kate said as she was licking her lips. "Anyone checked in on the kids and my parents this morning?"

Norman answered through a bite of waffle, "Checks were every two hours last night. I just talked to Brett this am. They are good."

Kate let out a sign of relief. She figured that whoever searched the house must have either found what they wanted or thought she didn't have it. Perhaps they wouldn't circle back. She hoped anyway.

"Jason, I figure we'll head out in 20," Mike said.

"Head out?" Kate asked.

"To Fort Benning. Mike has some buddies there who can help us with some information on our victim," Jason replied.

"Don't you think that's a little dangerous, given that I'm probably a murder suspect by now?" Kate questioned sarcastically.

"Actually, no. You're not. I checked the scanner this am. Police reports are that the church was a dead end." Mike replied.

"Wow. Ok, so they either didn't search my car or thought I was going to be hungry when I went hunting I suppose." Kate laughed.

"We don't know what the tip was. When I caught up with the chatter, the discussion was just about coming up empty, so it's possible the tip was real, but the car involved was not close to yours in color or style, so they didn't check it." Mike said.

"How do we get into the base?" Jason asked.

"Not a problem, guys. You are my guests," Mike replied.

Kate wondered if that was against the law. She didn't know the rule on civilians on army bases, although she probably should, given her background with security clearances. Then again, when she went on a military base as an investigator, she had a badge, so there was no reason for her to know that rule. Mike seemed like a standup guy, so if he said it was ok, then it must be. It's not like they had many options.

Kate finished her breakfast and went back to the guest room to pack the backpack. She asked Mike for a pen and paper to work through some thoughts on the ride. He obliged, and she ran downstairs to take a photo with the ipad of her "crime board" in the command center and scribble notes from the Excel file. They all climbed into Norman's Jeep and headed toward the main highway. Fort Benning was about 45 miles away which should have given Kate some time to work through a couple of theories on paper. Instead, she found herself doodling. She didn't have any theories. She took the blob she had been doodling and made a funny creature out of it. Seems she was much better at drawing than being a detective, and that wasn't saying much.

Chapter 13

Kate held her breath as they entered the gate at Fort Benning. The guards didn't seem to flinch at letting them in, although she wasn't sure what Mike had told the soldier at the gate. At this point, it didn't much matter; they were in. Norman drove the Jeep into the base and navigated to the administration building parking lot. Mike exited the Jeep and motioned for them to follow. And they did, all in a row like ducks.

As they walked to the building, Kate looked around at her surroundings, remembering her days as an investigator. She was never assigned to a case at Fort Benning, but it looked eerily like other bases she had visited. Red brick buildings with little architectural design. Manicured lawns with the rare flower bed. But there was plenty of activity around the base for a Saturday -- platoons moving from one building to another, Humvees driving around, and so forth. Mike made a call on his phone and a soldier appeared from inside the building. They greeted each other with a manly hug, and Norman gave the soldier a firm handshake. Mike introduced him as "Squirrel" to Jason and Kate, and although they both wanted to ask, they refrained from getting the backstory on that nickname. Kate was hoping this would prove fruitful.

Squirrel used his keycard to open the door and held it for the four of them to enter. "Now this isn't like the old days, Mike. You guys will have to wait in the lobby while I see what I can dig up on this guy. Security and all."

"Roger that," Mike replied. He handed Squirrel a piece of paper and motioned for the three of them to sit in the sterile chairs just to the left of the reception desk. The lobby walls were filled with paintings of famous battle scenes which fascinated Jason. No other décor was visible. The floor was an industrial tile, and the walls were white.

"These guys are going to wait for some information, Sarge," Squirrel noted to the man behind the reception desk.

The Sarge nodded, and Squirrel disappeared. Mike lingered at the desk to fill out the visitor log. Kate wasn't sure why she and Jason came along if they couldn't be part of the search, but then again, staying in the woods by themselves wasn't that appealing either. At least here she felt protected. She couldn't help but be disappointed that they weren't allowed back in the room where Squirrel was digging up information. That's not how it's done in the movies, she thought.

While they waited, Jason rambled on about the history behind all the paintings, and several men in uniform walked by tipping their hats to Mike. An older man who appeared to be a high-ranking officer by the look of the medals on his uniform approached him for conversation. Kate overheard Mike tell him that Squirrel was helping him with a PI case. Kate didn't know Mike was a PI. Come to think of it, Kate didn't know much about what Mike did, only what he used to do. And that was kill some terrorists in Afghanistan. She leaned toward Jason to confirm, "Mike is a PI?"

"Not full time. I think he dabbles in it to make extra money. He works on choppers now and is still on active reserve status."

"Is that how he's able to get these guys to pull information for us?" Kate asked Jason.

"Possibly. Mike's kind of a private man. I don't ask too much, but he's trustworthy, Kate. If someone gives him the info, I'm sure he has clearance for it," Jason said.

Kate didn't understand how Jason was friends with these guys and seemed to know so little about what they did. How could you have a friend and not know what he did for a living, she wondered. She turned her thoughts back to why they were there and wondered what type of information Mike asked for and how it could help them. After Mike wrapped up his conversation, Kate asked Mike, "Do you think I can use a phone here to call the kids?"

"Let's hold off on that for now. I don't have access to a secure line. My clearance isn't that high."

Kate squirmed in the chairs, as the side bars were pressing into her thighs. She wondered what was taking so long and what information they might get. She excused herself to the restroom twice, mostly to get out of the chair and burn off nervous energy. After about two hours, Squirrel returned with a manila folder and the original paper Mike gave him. "This is all I could find on your guy. If something else turns up, I'll give you a call."

"Thanks, Squirrel. I owe you, Man," Mike said as he shook Squirrel's hand.

"No problem. I hope you figure it out," Squirrel replied.

Mike moved toward the exit, and the three followed. Kate turned to give a smile and a half wave to Squirrel. "Thanks," she mouthed as they exited the building. The foursome returned to the Jeep in reverse formation as they entered, with Norman leading and Mike in the rear. As they approached the Jeep, Kate shivered and braced herself for the climb upward into the vehicle.

They sat for a minute waiting for instruction from Mike who was scanning the file.

"Anything useful?" Kate probed. She wanted to rip the file out of Mike's hands and read it for herself, but she forced herself to remember how grateful she was and sat on her hands instead.

"I'm not sure. Scott Brown wasn't just an investigator. He was a G-man all the way. Looks like he was rising in ranks in the FBI, and then quit one day to go be an investigator."

"That doesn't make any sense," Kate snapped, "why would a rising FBI agent give that up to be a lowly investigator?"

"I don't know. Why would a Georgia Tech graduate with a master's degree work at a movie theater?" Jason inserted. Jason's dig was directed at Kate, who had done just that. Kate had graduated at the top of her class from one of the best engineering schools in the country, although she was not an engineer. She had bounced around in her early career trying to decide what she wanted to be when she grew up. In addition to working in marketing, Kate had taught college, been an investigator and even managed a movie theater.

"Maybe the FBI wasn't all that," Kate offered, unamused at Jason's slam on her past choice of careers.

"Here, Kate, maybe you can see a pattern that will help us piece this together," Mike said as he offered her the file. "Let's grab some lunch around the corner at Sunny's."

Chapter 14

Kate scanned the file for any tidbits as the Jeep headed toward Sunny's, just off the base.

The four piled out of the Jeep, and Norman and Mike scanned the perimeter before entering the restaurant. Kate wasn't sure what they were looking for, but they were professionals, and it showed. Jason picked out a booth in the far corner of the restaurant with a clear view of the entire building and both entrances. Kate opened the file and tried to piece together parts of her life with Scott's. She was looking for any clue to shed light on this insanity she had wondered into in the last 48 hours.

The waitress brought menus and waters for the table and offered the specials. After they ordered, Kate excused herself to the restroom. Her tennis shoes squeaked and stuck to the floor as she entered the ladies' room. Mike rushed in front of her to check out the room before she entered as a precaution. Against what, Kate was clueless. She entered the room and locked it behind her. Tears started to fall again, and Kate was unsure why. The stress of the situation was getting to her. Kate wiped her eyes and washed her face. "Get it together," she thought. "Lord, help me figure this out. Save me from this, whatever it is. I can't do it without You."

Kate returned to their lunch and finished her meal. She was anxious to dig back into Scott Brown's file. Kate noticed that they were the only customers in the restaurant. She checked her watch. It was 10:45, so she figured the local lunch crowd must not have funneled in yet. Just as she was starting to read the file, Mike's phone buzzed with a text. "Guys, we need to move. Now!" Mike warned.

Jason grabbed Kate by the hand and pulled her to her feet. Her knee was still sore from the day before, and it took a minute to get going. Only from the sound of it, they didn't have a minute. Kate was unsure what was happening, but knew if Mike said move, he meant it. Kate grabbed $40 from her backpack and slapped it down on the table, hoping it was enough. They didn't have time to wait for the check.

The foursome headed for the door with Mike in front and Norman bringing up the rear, just like Jason had practiced in MAG training. They moved toward the Jeep quickly. Suddenly, a man in a black suit and tie clipped Mike's feet with a swift kick and landed on top of him. Kate snapped her head around just in time to see another man pulling Norman to the ground from behind. Jason and Kate started to run toward the Jeep but were cut off by two other men who towered over both her and Jason. Kate knew not to be taken, but she
100

didn't know how to fight these guys. They looked like they could drag her off without a problem. She looked back to see Mike and Norman on the ground with the men on top of them, holding them down. If Stone Cold Steve Austin couldn't win this fight, how was she going to? Kate darted to the left, and the man in her path stuck his arm out to hold her at arm's length by her shoulder and said, "Stop. We just want the file. Give us the file, and this all goes away."

The man was roughly 6"5" and had well defined muscles in his arm and legs that were showing through the suit he was wearing. Kate figured he could probably bench 350 pounds without breaking a sweat. She knew she couldn't out run the men, or out maneuver them. She was trapped. She closed her eyes and prayed, "Lord please give me wisdom and help me defeat Goliath."

"Kate," Jason shouted as the other man pinned him against a nearby SUV. "Let her go!"

Kate's lip quivered. She wasn't sure what to do. For an instance, she tried to think about all those silly shows and if any of them had a realistic scene of escape she could draw on. She quickly dismissed that thought as insane; after all, those were make believe! She looked over at Jason, hoping the man wouldn't hurt him before she figured out what to do.

"We know Scott gave you the file at the school on Thursday," the man stated gruffly. "Just give us the file, and we'll leave you alone."

Kate suddenly felt a wave of confidence come over her. God renewed her strength in that moment and gave her wisdom to see clearly. These guys were like the FBI agent. They had to be acting outside of the law, but they didn't want to do her harm, or they would have already snatched her. And the guys holding her friends hadn't drawn any weapons. Kate decided it was time for a red-headed temper tantrum. She channeled her best white trash trailer park voice and slapped the man's hand from her shoulder. She pointed her finger in his face, stepped forward, squinted her eyes and started in on him. "You know what that man you call Scott gave me on Thursday?" Kate reached into her backpack as the man flinched, unsure of her next move. He grabbed her arm as she came up with the flyer in her hand. He relaxed his grip after realizing it wasn't a weapon, and she snatched her hand away from him. She pushed the flyer in his face and railed, "A big fat fight with my kids over a trampoline place. Yeah, he got them all excited by giving me a flyer to a trampoline place, but the coupon he gave me doesn't work! I had to tell my kids we weren't going because those crazy people want $22 an hour for a kid to jump. My kids cried for an hour. So, when you find this Scott guy, you tell him I'm coming for him. No one messes with my kids. And for the record, that man cannot park. He nearly clipped my front end with his white trash Honda. Someone should take his license." Kate crumpled the flyer into a ball and dropped it at the feet of the man guarding her as she finished off her tirade, "Now if you will excuse me, I'm going to back to my friend's house to enjoy my one weekend with no whiny kids. Are we done here?"

The man didn't move. He seemed unmoved by her commanding performance but was clearly waiting for instructions from someone else. A man got out of the SUV next to her. "Let them go," he said.

The men in suits moved away from all four of them and retreated to their vehicle without a word. Jason moved toward Kate. "Yeah, you better go," she blurted out, still in character before realizing she might be pushing her luck a little much.

Jason grabbed her hand and squeezed, hoping his firm hand would be enough of a hint. Kate turned toward the man. He was the same FBI agent from the parking lot at work! Kate started to move toward him. She wanted to question him for a change, but Jason's grip got tighter, holding her in place.

"Don't," Jason said under gritted teeth.

Kate stood and watched the SUV pull out of the lot. Mike ran back inside the restaurant and returned momentarily. None of the employees saw the incident, and there weren't any parking lot cameras. Of course, Kate thought. No theft, no witnesses, no follow up from local police. Kate hoped her performance would be enough to throw them off the trail. She grabbed the flyer and climbed into the Jeep. They headed back down the highway toward Mike's place.

Jason leaned into Kate. "You ok?"

"Yeah, you?"

"Yeah. I guess sometimes it's ok to complain and gripe, huh? Your complaining sure served us well back there!" Jason joked.

"No hard feelings, Point Break, you got a mean swing," Kate said to Jason, quoting again from *The Avengers* and being very thankful for God's wisdom and strength.

"Woo, buddy. Jason, I'd hate to be you. Your woman can deal it out, can't she?" Norman joked.

"Hell hath no fury like a redhead scorned," Mike chimed in.

"No, it does not, so you boys better remember that or what just happened will seem like a cakewalk when I'm through with you," Kate said in her white trash character as she smiled, the adrenaline still rushing through her body. She couldn't believe that she stood up to that man or that it worked.

Jason had never actually been on the end of a such a tirade from Kate. Their relationship was anything but volatile. Kate was a reasonable woman, and Jason rarely gave her cause to be upset.

"That's 10 pounds of crazy in a 5-pound bag," Jason laughed as he quoted Elliot from *Leverage*.

"What is it with you guys and all the one-liners?" Norman asked.

"It's just this thing we do with each other," Jason said. "Hey, Mike, who were those guys?"

"They weren't Army folks, I can tell you that," Mike replied. "Looked like federal agents of some sort. They had earpieces in. And that SUV had government plates."

"Can we find out who they are?" Kate asked.

"Maybe," Mike answered.

"How did you know we needed to move?" Jason asked.

"Squirrel sent a scatter or splatter text after getting a notification that OPM file had a red flag on it. Must have alerted the wrong people. Squirrel ain't no rat, so I reckon the visitor log was enough to do us in. Sunny's isn't exactly hidden from view, and the log records our vehicle make/model and tag number," Mike answered.

"Scatter or splatter text?" Kate asked in a high-pitched voice. "Never mind. I don't even want to know."

"Think more are coming?" Jason asked.

"I doubt it. Usually those red flags are for extreme cases or if you pull your own file. With Scott Brown being deceased, that file would be accessed by a dozen different people to go along with pending investigations. My guess is that flag was put on the file by whoever is looking for the Excel file."

"The FBI agent," Kate figured. "We need to figure this thing out. If the FBI are involved it, we are in over our heads."

"That's the thing, though. I'm not so sure they are involved. Seems more like a rogue agent to me," Jason interjected.

"A rogue agent with a team of willing participants and government resources," Kate answered.

"They may not know the whole story, Kate. Chain of command and all still applies in the FBI. One thing is for sure; if they aren't willing to use the badge to intimidate a civilian into giving up information and are relying on fear of physical threat, there is more to that story than we are aware of. Either way, it was obvious they weren't prepared to do us harm, and that means something," Mike said.

"Yeah, I noticed they didn't pull out their weapons. That's kind of off, isn't it?" Kate asked. "I'm surprised they were able to get a jump on you and hold you down."

"Sometimes it doesn't matter how big or good you are. It's about position, timing, and leverage, and they had that on us," Mike said. "Doesn't mean I'm happy about it. It won't happen again."

Norman let go of the wheel with both hands and sent them flying into the air. "There's a second player!"

"What?" Jason yelled. "How do you know that?"

Mike turned to face Jason, "Because Scott Brown is dead, and we aren't."

"Bingo!" Norman yelled. "If that file is worth killing over, why did they let us go?"

Kate sunk in her seat. "Oh, man, you are right. And I thought it was because of my winning performance."

Jason joked, "Babe, you were great back there. Don't get me wrong – I don't ever want to be on the back end of that type of chewing, but you did great. And it worked. We just have to figure this out before the real bad guys find us."

"You don't think the FBI guy is a bad guy?" Kate asked.

"No," Mike answered.

"Why not? He has attacked me twice in two days," Kate shrieked.

"Look," Mike started to explain, "I'm not saying the guy is squeaky clean or anything, but if he was a real threat, we'd be dead by now. He's had more than one opportunity to cap you, Kate, and you don't even have a scratch. I think he's the mystery burglar in your house, too. He's not using that badge because he's not working officially on the case. We need to find out if he and Scott knew each other. He's working some angle, and your performance back there might have gotten him to forget about us for a while, but Norman's right. We have another player, who fortunately, hasn't figured out that you are part of the equation yet."

"Maybe this is where we get out, then. If the other player doesn't know Kate has the file, then maybe we just let it go and go back to our normal lives," Jason offered.

"It's a risk, man, to look over your shoulder for the rest of your lives, but it's your call," Mike answered.

Jason let Mike's words sink in for a minute. They had kids. No, letting it go wasn't an option, and he knew it. He glanced over at Kate and knew she was thinking the same thing.

"Get me to a computer. I know there is something I'm missing," Kate said.

Chapter 15

Once again, they entered Mike's property. Norman and Mike got out first and entered the house, weapons drawn. "Clear," Mike said from the left side of the house.

"Clear," Norman responded.

Kate and Jason got out of the Jeep and entered the house. Kate went straight to the command center and set up shop without saying a word to anyone.

"What's up with her?" Norman asked.

"Kate? Oh, she's on a mission. Just wait. You'll see. She's like a dog with a bone when she wants something done. Now that the imminent danger is gone in her mind, she'll do her thing. It's quite scary, actually." Jason warned.

"I want to beef up some of the security traps around here. I don't think our second player is messing around, so I want to be ready. I don't want a repeat of what just happened," Mike said. "Let me see if Squirrel can track that plate number and then we can get started."

"Let's do it," Jason agreed.

"Norman, you keep watch of the system while Jason and I work," Mike instructed.

"Roger that," Norman agreed.

Mike called Squirrel and then he and Jason headed to the shed to get supplies. Mike loaded Jason's arms with cables, wires and tools. Jason thought about Mike's time in Afghanistan. Setting a lethal trap wasn't beyond Mike's ability, or probably his mindset, but he wasn't sure he wanted to be part of it. Still, this was self-defense. Jason decided not to ask too many questions and just follow instructions.

Mike began rolling out wires, clamping them to various trees and spots in the yard. He covered them with foliage and dirt to hide anything visible. It was fascinating to watch him work, even if Jason wasn't sure what Mike was doing. Sweating in the cold started to get to Jason. He wasn't as fragile as Kate, but this was way more work than he was used to.

After about four and a half hours, Mike was sufficiently satisfied with their work. "That ought to do it," he mused, pleased with his work.

"Are any of these lethal?" Jason finally asked.

"Heck, no, brother. I'm not crazy. A man steps on my property he probably has it coming, but the good Lord much less the law wouldn't think too kindly of me taking it out on someone without due process. What makes you think I'd do something like that?"

"I don't know. I guess your background in the military?" Jason said, trying not to offend Mike.

"That type of work was a long time ago, and it had its purpose, Jason. Just because I can doesn't mean I should – remember the Apostle Paul's words in Corinthians. All things are lawful, but not all things are beneficial."

"Well, that's a relief. Kind of. But how exactly does all this protect us?"

"I said they weren't lethal. I didn't say anything about not hurting," Mike said with a smile.

By the time the guys came downstairs, Mike's command center had become Kate's command center. Kate was a clicker. And she typed nearly 120 words a minute. She had 24 tabs open on Chrome and was using 5 of the 8 screens. The white board looked like the blue and green markers exploded into WWIII. She was bent over writing feverishly on a notepad when they entered.

"Whoa! What have you done to my stuff?" Mike joked.

Kate had no time for games. She was in a groove. Still the stench that just entered the room got her attention. "Ick! You guys smell." Kate jerked back in the chair.

"That's the smell of a man working to protect his bride," Jason said proudly.

Kate had to chuckle at Jason's boast. He was such an old-fashioned man. He was a Southern Gentleman, through and through, from his insistence to opening doors to his thick Mississippi accent. Kate loved Jason's Southern charm. She often wondered how a man mired in chivalry could love such a go-getter as her. And yet, she secretly wanted to be doted on; she just didn't know how to let him do it.

Kate started rattling off theories and ideas as quickly as they popped into her head and without taking a breath.

"He was my instructor at the Mine! I didn't remember him until I read the file again. The job history isn't that detailed, but one of his coworkers mentioned he was an instructor at US Investigations. I only remember one person from that class anyway – Susan Pierson -- and that's only because we are Facebook friends. I'm not sure how he found me, but that's the link. I was his top investigator. I remember Susan teasing me about it a couple of years ago; that I was his favorite, most frustrating trainee ever. I thought she was just kidding around, but maybe I was. The dyslexia thing has to be on purpose, though. Scott Brown wouldn't have made it into the FBI or to write reports as an investigator unless he had conquered that disability, and I certainly don't remember him having it. I originally thought the first email was a post office box number, but we all know how that turned out. OPM badges are four-digits so if you assume that the letters are rearranged from the on-purpose dyslexia, then I think POMB #1257 could be OPM Badge #1257. I don't know how to identify who has that badge, though. All the interviewees in Scott's file say he left the FBI on good terms, but they don't know why. The history doesn't go back that far, so we only have testimony of those interviewed. Only one guy speculates what it might have been. He says Scott was angry when he got told to sideline a case that he had worked for months. According to the testimony in the file, Scott had a smoking gun and was told to stand down. The next day, the case was closed. And check this out. It took some digging but look who this is." Kate pulled one of the open windows forward to reveal a picture of the FBI agent they all saw earlier in the day.

"That's him! That's the FBI guy!" Jason shouted.

"Whoa, whoa, whoa! Wait a minute! I need a minute to process all of what Kate just said. Man, that was a mouthful," Norman said.

"Told you she was on a mission," Jason joked. "Who is the FBI guy, Kate?"

"John Schaeffer. He's married to this woman here, who is related to Scott Brown." Kate pointed to a beautiful blonde in the picture.

"Ok, how did you do that?" Norman asked, impressed.

"Age of the geek, baby," Jason quoted from *Leverage*, one of his favorite shows to watch with Kate. Kate let out a bellowed laugh as Jason leaned down to kiss her.

Kate continued, speaking as rapidly as before and with sheer glee of solving part of the mystery, "Scott's family started an online memory book this morning for his funeral. Out of town and close family is usually the first to respond online. I had to go through about 45 different posts and search for their information, but eventually I found Mrs. Schaeffer's. She posted pictures of her and Scott as young adults. They were close until she moved down here with her husband. I looked up her online profile on Facebook and found she was married to John and recently posted about – get this – how angry she was her husband didn't win an award he deserved this week at work. I'm sure that's why he was at the award ceremony at our church, only he didn't get the award. She doesn't mention that he's an agent, but that's not surprising given the public nature of the internet. I searched public records in Cobb County to find they own a home in Brookstone, just around the corner from the school and our house."

"That's pretty cool," Norman said.

"Are you thinking our FBI agent is trustworthy, Kate?" Jason asked.

"Maybe. I'm not sold on that yet, but not ruling it out. Mrs. Schaeffer says she didn't know Scott was in town, which means she hadn't seen him, or won't admit to it. Either of those throws up at least a yellow flag for me. The Kennesaw Neighbor's story of the murder states Scott had been in town on vacation for a week to visit family when he was killed. So far, I haven't found any other family in the area, but it's not like I have his entire family tree to work with here, and that could have been an excuse to stop questions about whatever he was really doing. But if Scott was working with the FBI, I would think he'd drop in on his old pal, right?"

"Maybe he thought it was too dangerous to involve Mrs. Schaeffer." Jason offered.

"That's certainly plausible," Kate conceded. "From the pictures I found, it looks like they were close, at least at one point. Maybe he wanted to protect her."

"Her husband is an FBI agent. She has to be used to the life," Norman interjected.

"Perhaps, but her online Facebook profile is public. Kind of strange for someone who is used to danger. I mean, even mine isn't public," Kate argued.

"Maybe it's more that she's not terrible tech savvy," Jason said.

"Could be. A lot of people don't realize the privacy settings or remember to adjust them," Kate said.

Mike had been listening intently the whole time, thinking about what was going on. He wasn't an educated man by the world's standards, but he had more experience with this type of scenario than anyone else in the room. "When did the Schaeffer's buy that house?"

"2014," Kate replied.

"And are there other pictures of Mrs. Schaeffer and Scott together in 2012 or 2013 or any after 2014" Mike asked.

"Let me check," Kate said as she started scrolling through the timeline of Amelia Schaeffer. "A lot before 2014, but I don't see any after that. Facebook clips posts in the timeline, though, especially that far back, so there could some I'm not seeing, although if they were that close, I would think at least one would pop up in the timeline."

"Ok, look. Let's assume Scott left the FBI over some moral issue and moved to be an investigator, looking to right a wrong. He finally finds something. He's not going to go to his buddies in the FBI in Virginia because they can't be trusted or are long gone. Mrs. Schaeffer and Scott Brown were close until the move down here in 2014." Mike started.

Jason finished the thought, "So he decides to come down here and give the file to his old buddy and relative, the FBI agent deserving of some award."

"Then how did the file end up with me?" Kate asked. "He had plenty of time to get it to Schaeffer since he had been in town a week."

Silence fell on the room.

"I know! I know!" Kate screamed. "Scott didn't have the file yet, that's why! He's not the one with dyslexia either. He came down here to get the file and then hand it off to his FBI buddy once he had it." Kate exclaimed.

"It's a little bit of a stretch, don't you think, Kate?" Norman asked.

"No, think about it. He doesn't know the area, and he's carrying around a flyer to a local trampoline place with a secret message embedded in it. How would he know about that place ahead of time? So, he retrieves the flyer from his contact and heads toward Brookstone to give it to John, but maybe he feels threatened or followed and stops at the school. For some reason, he decides to dump the flyer in a panic, but it's too late.

He's killed just behind the school after our encounter."
Kate finished it off with a "Ta-da!"

"Why did he give you the password?" Mike asked.

"UGGH! Did you have to shoot a bazooka through my big reveal?" Kate grumbled.

"Things aren't always as nice and tidy as our detective shows on television, Kate," Jason said,

"Yeah, but this feels way too much like an episode of Law and Order where they don't resolve the crime. I hate that show. You spent an hour watching something you want to know it was settled, and the bad guys were caught," Kate complained.

"Kate," Jason said supportively, "I love you, but you know it's only been 48 hours, right? Give yourself a break. Think about what you've endured over the last 2 days. The fact that you gotten this far is amazing in and of itself."

"But I have to solve this!" Kate argued. She could feel the tears swelling as she swallowed hard. She was so mad at herself for not being able to push this to a conclusion. This wasn't a television show. It was her life, and results mattered.

"Hey, your theory isn't dead. Just because we don't know why you wound up with the file and the password doesn't mean it's without merit. We still have to figure out what the file is and where to take it to finish this.

Let's take a break, get cleaned up and have some dinner, and then we'll come back to it," Mike offered.

"I miss my kids. Is it safe to call them?" Kate asked.

"Let's hold off on phone calls a little while longer. Brett said all was quiet at your house, but I'd hate to stir up trouble. What about an email?" Mike offered. "Phone calls can be overheard or intercepted."

"What about emails?" Kate asked, "You don't think some punk in his mom's garage can hack an email server?"

Jason busted out laughing. "Yeah, probably the same guy that got Hilary's emails is just waiting to take us out. Hey, Kate, now is when that nerdy ham radio stuff comes in handy, by the way."

"Yeah, you can re-task a NASA satellite, you can get a level 3 security clearance, but you can't hack a hick," Kate quipped.

Jason smiled, revealing his dimples, but Norman and Mike were not amused. They clearly didn't get the reference to *Leverage*.

"Ok, a text, from someone else's phone? Mom knows mine is lost. Can they trace locations from text messages?" Kate asked.

"Who knows what they can do these days. That sounds like a fair risk, if we turn the phone off right after. Let's use Carmon's; I'll get it." Mike answered.

"Who's Carmon?" Kate whispered.

"Mike's wife. She's in Mexico for the month," Jason replied.

Kate had assumed he was divorced or widowed. He had never heard Jason speak about Carmon before. And from the looks of the house and the lack of girlie paraphernalia, her presence wasn't commanding in this household.

Mike emerged and handed the phone to Kate, "Just a quick note, no detail about what you are doing or anything that can give our location away. Turn the phone off when you are done."

Kate thought long and hard about the text. Her mind drifted as she stared at the floor. She smiled thinking about how many popsicles Logan had conned out of Grandma by now. Logan often got the short end of the stick being Landon's younger brother because of attention Kate had to pay to Landon to keep him on track, but he was a smart kid. He was witty and brave, and he loved to eat. Landon was scared of his own shadow, but he loved his momma. He could be the sweetest boy sometimes. Tears fell once again onto Kate's cheeks. She could taste the salt as they hit her lips. She fell to her knees and cried out, "Jesus, I am calling on you now. I need you every hour of every day, and never more have those words been true than today. I'm not sure what mess we are in, but I have faith you are able to lead us through this dark hour. Give us wisdom, strength, and courage through the power of the Holy Spirit and deliver us from this evil," she prayed. Kate wiped her eyes and typed "Hey, it's me. Still haven't found my phone, so I borrowed one. These goofballs are wearing me out. Kiss the boys for me. Love you!" She hit send and turned off the phone.

Chapter 16

"Do we know who the investigator leaked it to?" Jack asked beating his fist on the table.

"Not yet, sir," Benny answered. "But I have my best guys on it."

"If you had taken care of this when I said this wouldn't have been a problem," Jack barked.

"Rocco assured me he did," Benny said.

"Took care of it? You think he took care of it? He didn't even make sure the guy was dead!" Jack said sarcastically.

"Well, he's dead now," Benny responded.

"And we still don't know where that file is because of your numskull professional. No more excuses, Benny. Find out and take care of it, or our careers are over. That file can't get out."

Benny exited the small office and went back to the bullpen. All his guys were working furiously, but that wasn't good enough. "Pull up the movements again of Schaeffer and Johnson and put them on the big screen," Benny barked out. He stared at the screen looking for a clue. "He's hiding something, and I need to know what it is."

"Jason, did you cross reference all the employees at that factory with the other five locations of our investigator and Schaeffer?" Benny asked.

"Yeah, boss, but it's thin. The only match is this woman," Jason said pointing to Kate's picture on the screen. She works at the factory and has kids that attend the school. No direct connection to our guy or Schaeffer, though."

"Well, where is she?" Benny asked.

"Not sure, sir." Jason answered.

"Anyone been to her house?" Benny asked angrily. "Tell me someone has been to her house!"

"Yeah, boss. Marco checked it out. She's not there, but there is some activity at the house that shares the driveway. Looks like some redneck convention. We were staked out there for a few hours, but no sign of the woman since we identified her, so we pulled resources back to work Schaeffer's other locations. We've double checked all known associates for the woman, and no leads there."

"Come on, guys! I need something to work with here!" Benny Barked.

"Got something!" a voice yelled above the crowd.

Benny rushed over to the see. The man who found something was new to the DEA, so Benny was pleased he was having success so quickly.

"Look here. This is that same woman leaving Fort Benning, where the OPM file of our investigator was pulled. She's with someone in our database," the man said. "A Mike Cutter, Ranger. Lives in Pine Mountain with his wife and son."

"Excellent! Jason, find out where his house is and get Crenshaw on the phone. I don't want this one on the books."

Chapter 17

Dinner was ready. Mike and Norman had spent time harassing each other about who cooked a better steak. Jason knew the answer, and it wasn't either of them. He had that locked down. Still, the meal was edible. Kate barely spoke or laughed at the jokes. Jason knew her mind was busy working the case, so he didn't push it.

"Did you find out about the plates of the SUV from the restaurant?" Kate asked.

"Not much. Registered to FBI, which we knew. That's all Squirrel could get," Mike answered.

Kate frowned. She didn't know what to do. She put her hand up to her temple and stared aimlessly at her plate, pushing the meat slowly around in a circle.

"Hey, why don't you take a bath in Mike's whirlpool tub and see if you can work the rest of that stress out of your head," Jason offered.

"Yeah, bubbles might help me break the case wide open," Kate quipped back sarcastically, and then instantly regretted snapping at Jason. "But it does sound nice," she said, trying to make up with Jason. She shrugged her shoulder and gave a half smile, hoping he would understand her hidden and lame excuse for an apology. "Do you mind, Mike?"

"Not a bit," Mike replied. "Come on, and I'll show you the ropes."

Kate suddenly remembered she didn't have any clean clothes to put on. "Can we borrow the washing machine, too?"

"Jason put your clothes in the wash last night before turning in. I think he got them out after his shower. I'll have him bring them in to you." Mike said. Jason was really shining during this crisis, Kate thought.

Mike grabbed a towel for Kate and asked if she needed anything else before leaving Kate to her bubble bath. Jason brought her clean clothes in and gave her a quick kiss. "We'll figure this out," he said as he left the room.

Kate ran the water as hot as she could stand it and climbed in the tub. She knew getting out would be the challenge with her knee. She looked down and saw that it was still swollen. She hoped the water would help it. She turned the jets on and leaned her head back against the wall. Her mind was blocked with thoughts of how she got into this mess, and she knew that she had to push those aside in order to figure out how to get out of it. Questions raced in her head of possible reasons why she wound up with that flyer. Was it random? How could it be since he was her instructor? Why wouldn't he just turn the file over to his FBI friend? Why couldn't she find the answer?

Suddenly a pop shook the room. The bubbles stopped, and the lights went out.

Kate took a deep breath. It wasn't completely dark outside, as the moon was shining. After her eyes adjusted she could see a faint outline of things in the room. She started to call out but remembered that would be a dead giveaway of where she was if there was trouble. "Don't be that stupid woman, Kate." She told herself. The guys knew where she was. If it was nothing, someone would knock on the door and let her know. If it was something else, she'd know soon enough. Kate sat still and silent hoping it was just a breaker that popped. She tried to scan the room for anything that might be of use in case of a problem. Who was she kidding? She was in the dark in an unfamiliar house. Worse, she was naked in a tub with a busted knee. Kate heard footsteps and a caught the flicker of a flashlight shine across the door frame. Something was terribly wrong. Should she stay where she was? No, she couldn't die naked in the tub, but if she moved the water would slosh, and it wouldn't be hard to find her. And what was she going to do when she got out? Kate knew she was helpless, which is exactly where she did not want to be. Ever. She closed her eyes and asked for help from God. "Please don't let me die naked in another man's tub, Lord."

There was a large clatter in the other room followed by pots and pans banging. She knew her chance to move was now while any noise she made could be covered by whatever was happening in the house. She didn't have a plan, but getting out of that tub was important to her. She rolled to her stomach and awkwardly pushed to all fours, slinging her right leg with the arthritic knee over one side of the tub. Just as her foot reached the tile floor, the clatter stopped. Kate froze. Great, how long could she hold this pose, she wondered. She could feel her knee about to give, but her left hand slid on the tub floor first. She banged her head on the side of the tub and made a loud splash as she landed nearly upside down in the tub. Just the thing she was trying to avoid. The door knock nearly scared her to death.

"Kate?" Mike yelled.

Relief. One of the good guys. "Yeah?" Kate answered, "everyone ok?"

"Kate, we need to go." Mike's voice was stern.

Kate picked herself up and climbed out of the tub. She grabbed her clothes from the counter and tried to dry off quickly with what she hoped was the clean towel Mike laid out. She hit the high spots, as she knew time was of the essence. She couldn't make out much in the dark but managed to get her clothes on. The places she missed drying off were obvious in how her clothes stuck to her. She unlocked the door and emerged to find Jason standing at the door ready to lead her out of the house. He grabbed her hand and pulled her down the dark and narrow hallway shining his flashlight ahead of them. He kept asking if she was ok as they moved out the front door toward the Jeep.

"I'm fine. How about everyone else? What happened?" she asked.

"We're all good," Jason answered. "What, are you scared of a little thunder?"

Kate took the bait and quoted back from *The Avengers,* "I'm not overly fond of what follows." Kate climbed into the Jeep and sighed, waiting to hear what happened. Jason handed Kate her socks and tennis shoes.

"What? No stilettos for the big escape?" Kate joked. Kate constantly complained about television shows and movies that put female cops in heels in the field. She never understood how that was practical or believable, as heels were the single most uncomfortable thing on the planet, and no one was good at running in them. She wasn't much of a feminist, but it bothered her that only beautiful, tall, skinny models were cops on television. Real women never made it to the tube or the big screen.

"Well, they didn't have them in red," Jason said as he smiled at her. "I'm surprised at how calm you are."

"Calm? You know me, sarcasm helps settle me in a crisis. I wouldn't exactly call this calm, but I'd probably be freaking out more if I hadn't already run the worst scenarios through my mind, the least of which involved my parents seeing a news report of their dead, naked daughter straddling the side of a strange man's tub."

"That would be a bit difficult for me to explain to your parents," Jason replied, smiling at her. "I think your shirt is on backwards."

"Look, I'm lucky it's on at all," Kate huffed, pulling her arms inside the shirt and turning it to the right side.

The moonlight hit Kate's face and Jason gasped. "Your head is bleeding! What happened?"

"Oh, is it? I was on my way to take out some thugs when gravity intervened," Kate joked and grabbed at her head to see how much blood was really there. She was relieved to find it wasn't much. "Remind me to reenact the graceful exit from the tub for you later. I'm clearly going to have to work on my dismount if I want to take home the gold."

Jason could only imagine what had happened. He knew Kate struggled with her knee and getting up from a sitting position with help on dry land sometimes was a challenge, but to do it under duress in the dark with a slick surface, well, he imagined there had to be some serious adrenaline pushing his wife's exit. He was proud of her effort, though, and glad she appeared to be physically ok. She wasn't much on grace, but Jason noted that she was mentally stronger than they both realized.

Norman climbed in the Jeep and peeled out of the spot, heading to the main road.

"Wait! Where's Mike?" Kate yelled.

Just then, Mike sprinted out of the house and made an impressive leap onto the moving Jeep. "Go, go, go!" Mike ordered as he managed to stand on the running boards, open the door and climb in while Norman drove down the bumpy driveway. It was like a stunt from one of her shows. Mike had a cut on his face over his eye and was holding his left arm, but he looked relatively unscathed.

"You good, Man?" Norman asked.

"100%, Man. Did you see that sucker light up like a Christmas tree?" Mike relished, obviously wired from the encounter. He smiled from ear to ear.

"Oh yeah. Made my job easy. He wasn't going no where after that Griswold special. Fry 'em and tie 'em." Mike and Norman did a hi-five. "Hey, Man, what was that little one packin'?"

"9mm pistol. Took me about 3 seconds to take that away, but the dude had some Kung Fu moves. I mean, he ain't no Bruce Lee or nothing, but he had some moves." Mike recounted.

"You beat him with that jiu jitsu mess or straight up muscle?" Norman asked.

"What do you think, Man? It was all muscle. Like I'm going to let some 150-pound weakling have the satisfaction of a spar with me. I just put him down and put the ties on."

Kate was unclear what happened, but she was enjoying listening to these guys boast over their victory. "Hey, I don't want to break up your man party, but anyone want to let us in on what happened back there?" Kate interrupted.

"Oh, sorry, y'all," Mike started. "Some tangos tripped the security alarm. I told you no one gets past that system without me knowing. I sent Jason to guard your door and Norman outside to investigate. We verified it was just two tangos, so we sat back and waited. Norman's guy stepped on that trip wire we set earlier. I rigged it with some serious wattage. That's why the lights went out. Mine hit the trap in the kitchen making all that noise. I think every pan and knife missed him on the pull, but the distraction made it easy to get the jump on him. Hey, Norman, did you call it in?"

"Oh yeah, Sheriff Jones is going to be happy about that present we left. I bet they have records. He'll give us a heads-up once they are processed."

"Who were they?" Jason asked.

"My guess? The second party. The lethal one." Mike answered.

"The boys!" Kate screamed. "If they found us, what's to keep them from finding my parents and kids?"

"Don't worry, Kate. I let Sheriff Jones know to coordinate with the Cobb Police to send a team out for protection. He's a good man. Our guys are still staked out at your house, too. I talked to Brett a minute ago, and they beefed up security already." Norman answered.

"Send Kevin in to talk to Kate's dad before the cops show up. He's the best with that type of thing," Jason noted.

"Copy that," Mike said. "Norman, keep going straight on this highway. I'll let you know when we get close." Mike grabbed Norman's phone to make the call with instructions for Kevin. He wasn't thrilled with having to use a cell phone that might be tracked, but so far, Norman seemed like the one part of the group that hadn't been connected. Mike assumed his phone was safest for communication at this point.

"Kevin," Mike started. "You got the debrief on the current situation?" Mike paused for the answer. "Alright good. You deliver the news about the new friendlies coming by. Leave the family in the dark as much as possible - when it doesn't interfere with safety. We're moving to alt plan Bravo, location Delta and will be available on comms after about midnight. Checks on the hour from now on." Mike paused again. "Roger that." Mike hung up the phone and turned to Kate and Jason. "No movement at the house. Everyone is safe. Cops just arrived, and Brett intercepted them. Your family is in good hands now."

Kate breathed a little sign of relief, but still was concerned. She knew she had to trust them, but she was terrified that there would be someone coming after her family. She had to figure this out and get it solved quickly. She wondered what alt plan Bravo and location Delta were. She figured the comms had to be the ham radios. So maybe planning for the apocalypse had its advantages, Kate thought. She started to ask about their code plans and locations when Jason announced,

"While I was downstairs another email came in on Kate's address."

"What did it say?" Kate asked.

"I don't know. I didn't have time to read it before we were interrupted."

"Norman, can I borrow your phone to check it?" Kate asked.

Norman handed the phone to Kate, and she began to log into her email through his web browser. She clicked the email with the subject: Red Tiger and Xdrenline: A special offer from one of our partners. There was a logo of a Chinese restaurant – Red Tiger - and the words, "Bring this in for a free gift with purchase." The address looked to be next door to the trampoline place.

"That's it? No secret decoder ring?" Kate yelled at the phone. "I need a decoder ring! How am I going to figure out what this file is if you don't give me the key? Whoever set this up is on my last nerve." Kate wasn't much on patience, and this trickling of information was about to push her over the edge.

Jason leaned over and looked at the screen. "Maybe the free gift IS the decoder ring."

"You guys watch way too many spy shows." Norman chimed in.

"Yeah, we do. But this isn't a spy show. It's real, and I need a decoder ring." Kate started to cry. "If we don't figure this out, I might not be a mom for much longer."

"Don't go there, Kate. You know who is in charge. God's got this." Jason comforted her.

"Yeah, well, He may have it, but I don't." Kate snapped back. "Where are we going, anyway?"

"To switch cars, just in case, and then to a safe house," Mike announced.

"And they said *we* watched too many spy movies," Kate whispered to Jason, impressed with the level of thought this group had taken to prepare. Maybe they weren't all geeks after all, she thought.

With Mike's direction, Norman pulled the Jeep pulled into a dark driveway off the main highway and parked it under a shed behind a two-story house. The four exited the vehicle.

"Did you get the backpack?" Kate asked.

"Yeah, but I didn't have time to pack it. Just grabbed it as it was," Jason answered. Kate knew that meant she had money and passports but no extra clothes. Her other set of clothes was in the floor of Mike's bathroom where she left them. She hoped this would wrap up before she really needed another set of clothes anyway.

Chapter 18

Mike pulled a nearby tarp down in front of the door of the shed, concealing the Jeep. A dark-skinned man emerged from the shadows and approached Mike. "Here, brother. It's gassed up and ready to go."

"And the location?" Mike asked.

"I'll take care of it. They are on vacation until next weekend. You got lucky on that one," the man answered.

"Thanks, Sam. I owe you one." Mike answered, taking the keys from the man and moved toward a black Dodge Ram. Mike motioned to everyone to get in and tossed the keys to Norman, whom Mike clearly had designated as the driver.

Kate's curiosity got the better of her. "Who is Sam?" she asked as she climbed into the truck.

"Just a friend," Mike answered.

That answer wasn't very satisfying to Kate's need for information, but she'd have to live with it, as Mike didn't seem inclined to give her anything more, including where they were headed.

The Dodge Ram was quieter than the Jeep as it sped down the highway toward whatever mystery safe house was next on the list. Mike barked out directional orders to Norman from time to time as Kate's mind raced with theories and fears. She started plotting out what to do next.

Jason's head fell over against the glass of the window. Kate couldn't believe he was snoring. How could he sleep? She didn't bother to wake him. At least one of them could get some rest.

"He's sawing some logs back there, ain't he?" Mike said softly.

Kate smiled back and nodded in agreement.

Norman's phone rang about 11:15 pm. The sheriff was calling to update Norman on what he found out. His phone was louder than Mike's, and she could mostly hear the other side of the conversation. Kate leaned forward and concentrated.

"Hey, Norm. I don't have much for you. Your perps aren't doing much talking. Thomas Malcom and Frank Crenshaw are their names. The big one mouthed off about the DEA coming to get 'em. You know anything about that?"

"The DEA? Not the FBI?" Norman asked.

"No, he said DEA. Wanted us to call the head honcho but wouldn't tell us what official business they had. I'm not buying it. The little one has a record for B & E from

136

2012. We can hold them until the judge orders an arraignment hearing."

"Ok, thanks, Sheriff."

None of that made much sense to Kate. Why would the DEA be after them? She filed that information in her brain and kept trying to solve the mystery with the parts she understood. The hum of the tires provided much needed white noise for Kate to get lost in her own thoughts. She had been on such a roll earlier and now with this new email and the DEA involvement, she wasn't sure what to make of things. One thing was for certain, she had to get to the Red Tiger restaurant tomorrow.

They pulled into another long driveway about 11:45 pm and parked in the garage of a two-story brick house. Kate had been busy thinking when they were driving and was disoriented with where they were. She knew they must be well north of Mike's place, but she didn't know for certain. She thought she saw water as they entered the property, but it was dark and late, and she was tired. Mike got out of the truck and closed the garage door behind them. He motioned for them to stay in the truck while he checked the house with Norman. Once they were sure it was all clear, Mike motioned for them to come in the house.

Kate nudged Jason, "Hey, sleepy head."

Jason was startled by her touch and waved his hands as if to defend himself before realizing it was Kate. They both laughed out loud and got out of the truck. Jason brought the backpack in and helped Kate up the stairs. The tub dismount had jarred her knee, causing more swelling. She hobbled into the house but stopped suddenly causing Jason to run into the back of her. The décor was the exact opposite of Mike's house. The kitchen was painted a burnt orange color and had lavish granite countertops. A stainless-steel gas stove and double oven stood to the left of the fridge. The cabinets were cherry with raised panels and decorative knobs. Set with turquoise and yellow dishes, red napkins and purple glasses, the 6-top kitchen table was a high-boy.

Kate imagined a professional designer worked on this house. Either that or one of those stay-home moms with more money and time than she knew what to do with. She tried not to get distracted by jealousy and just be thankful for a place to stay.

"Welcome to location Delta, folks," Mike said with a smile and outstretched arms.

"Mike, how do you know they won't find us here?" Kate asked.

"I'm not connected in any way to this house or the truck, either on paper or by way of known associates. It's a convoluted story, and the more you know, the less secure the story is, so I'll just leave it at that. You'll just have to trust me." Mike answered.

Kate was again displeased at the lack of information but had to respect Mike. He has done nothing but do her favors and save her life the past two days. She thought she could give him a break. At least until she could try to figure out the connection herself once all this was over. Kate couldn't let a thread like that go un-pulled; it just wasn't in her nature.

"Jason, you guys can take the master on this one – it's around the corner to your right. There are two other bedrooms for us. This house is bigger than mine, so we have plenty of room to stretch out. I'm going to set up shop in the living room."

"Ok, thanks," Jason replied. He and Kate followed the corner around to the bedroom. It was a sage green color with coffered ceilings and crown molding painted stark white. The contrast in colors was nice, Kate thought. The bed was a hi-boy with a fluffy comforter and plenty of pillows. It was very feminine in style, and Kate figured that is why Mike didn't want the room. She looked in the master bath attached to the bedroom and saw a huge walk-in shower with all kinds of nozzles and buttons. The black marble counters capped off the medium brown with cabinet doors that boasted raised insets. The floor had a beautiful diamond pattern with decorative tile accents. Kate thought the faucet handles should have been brushed nickel instead of brushed gold, but the room was lavish and beautiful. She especially liked the ceiling fan in the master bath. She'd file that away as an idea for later.

"Wow," Kate said as she exited the bathroom and fell backwards on the bed. She stretched her arms out and sighed as she looked at the decorative ceiling.

"Long day, huh? How is your knee?" Jason asked.

"I'm ok. My head hurts, but I'll live," she answered. Jason immediately pulled out ibuprofen from the backpack pocket and handed them to her. Normally, Kate would protest, but she was tired and hurting. She swallowed the pills while still on the bed. She grabbed the knee brace from the backpack and slipped it on. It didn't exactly fit like it was supposed to, but compression helped her knee.

"I'm going to see if Mike is ready to get started yet," Jason said.

"Ok, help me up, and we'll go together," Kate answered.

Jason pulled Kate off the bed and gave her a quick hug and a kiss before they went back into the living area where Norman and Mike had set up shop. There was considerably less equipment than at Mike's house, but there were some screens and a laptop that Mike had already turned on to begin his work.

"All is quiet at your house and here," Mike noted.

"Great!" Jason answered.

"Ok, so now what?" Norman asked.

"We can go to bed and rest or stay up and work this out," Mike said.

"After what happened at your place, I'm not sleeping right now; you guys?" Kate quickly answered.

A resounding "no" came from Norman and Mike. Jason stayed quiet.

"Ok, so what do we know?" Mike started. "Scott Brown, former FBI, was an investigator for OPM and passed a file to Kate just before he was killed.

Jason interjected, "Ok, wait. What is OPM anyway?"

In unison, Mike and Kate answered, "Office of Personnel Management."

Jason grinned as Mike continued, "There is a connection with Kate and Scott from years ago at OPM, but we don't know why he passed the file to Kate rather than the FBI. An FBI agent that was related to Scott Brown is interested in the file enough to scare Kate but not desperate enough to harm her. Someone involved with the DEA knows about the file and has the ability to track Kate to me and my house, but we don't know how. We have a file with raw data and no key to decipher it, but 3 emails from another source who is providing the file."

"We need to find the source of the file," Norman said.

"How are we going to do that? Unless they teach hacking in apocalypse prepping 101, I think that is a tall order," Kate snapped. She was clearly tired and sarcasm was her method of dealing with the crisis. Jason shot her a look of disapproval. "What?" she snapped. "You know I'm right."

Mike brought his hand up to squeeze the bridge of his nose and rub his forehead. "We don't have the skills to figure out who set up the website or is sending the emails," Mike noted.

"So let's go to the Xdrenaline place and see if we can shake some leaves loose," Norman said waving his hands in the air, clearly frustrated with the slow pace of this. "Someone has to know something. Just give me 5 minutes alone with them. I can get them to talk."

"Who are you going to squeeze? We have no way of knowing if there is a connection with that place and the source," Jason noted. "I can see it now: Two militant white men beat up black teen employees at trampoline park. Film at 11."

"What about the DEA connection? Mike, is there anyone you know that can help us with that?" Kate asked.

"Not if they don't work for the DEA. That's a branch I'm not tight with," Mike answered. "We'll have to wait on Sheriff Jones on that one to see how it plays out."

"Then I think we have to go to the Chinese restaurant and see if there is a secret decoder ring for our file," Kate said.

"Could be a trap," Norman said.

"I don't think it's a trap. None of the other emails have led us into a trap. We really are at a dead end if we don't try to get this next clue," Kate argued.

"She's right, guys. We have to follow the bread crumbs. We can only hide out for so long, and we really don't have any more leads," Jason chimed in.

Mike said, "Let's do it. But then we have to find someone to give this information to that can make sense of it."

"Like who?" Jason asked.

There was a pause in the conversation while everyone looked at Kate. She knew the answer but didn't want to utter it. Finally, she sighed and said, "Our FBI friend."

Mike nodded in agreement. "He's not going to hurt you, Kate. He would have done it already."

"Well, someone tried to hurt us," Kate protested. "How do we know Schaeffer didn't send them? We saw earlier that he has allies who are capable."

"We don't, but if those goons from last night were asking for the DEA, then they probably aren't tied to our FBI agent. I wouldn't think there would be a lot of love lost between those two agencies," Jason offered.

"And if we don't do something, whoever is after us is eventually going to figure out a way to get to us. We can only hold our locations for so long. They'll get restless and start going after our families," Norman interjected. The room went cold.

Kate couldn't allow that kind of thought to distract her. It was too much to consider. Jason leaned over and squeezed her hand. He shot her a stern look and said, "Don't, Kate. Don't do that to yourself."

Kate blinked and pushed the tears down her face. Not her kids! Not her parents! She was not going to let them become victims while she hid out over some file she didn't even know what it was. She had to finish this. "Ok, let's say we give the file to Schaeffer. How do we know that he's not on the wrong side of this?"

"I think he is on the wrong side, but not the killing side, and that makes him an ally," Mike answered.

"Are you trying to say the enemy of my enemy is my friend?" Kate asked.

"Sort of. I'm not sure it is that clean, but you get the point. I can take the file to him if you are afraid, Kate," Mike answered.

Kate responded quickly, "No. This is something I have to do. We do it my way, though. Deal?"

"Deal," Mike answered.

Kate wasn't sure what her way was, exactly, but it felt good to pretend she was in charge and knew what to do given the past two days of being completely out of control.

"Mike, you on first over watch?" Norman asked.

"Yeah, it's my turn. Everyone else get some rest," Mike answered.

144

Kate and Jason retreated to the bedroom and started to turn down the bed. As she rounded the corner of the bed and headed for the bathroom, Jason said, "I think it's big enough for both of us."

"What is?" Kate asked.

"The huge walk-in shower. I wonder what all those nozzles do."

"Yeah, looks pretty cool, but remember I just got out of the tub when the trouble started at Mike's. I doubt I need to get clean again."

"Who said anything about getting clean?"

"Touché," Kate answered. "The hot water will help me relax anyway." Kate moved the backpack to an easy to grab location. Not wanting a repeat of earlier, she arranged the towels in a space on the counter that was easy to reach. Happy with her preparation, she undressed and entered the shower.

Chapter 19

Mike left his post in the living room to do a routine check around the property. As he walked to the back deck, he could smell the water from the lake just down the hill from the house. Thankful Aaron was on vacation this weekend, Mike took a deep breath and listened carefully for any unusual sounds. He was pleased to hear none.

After three tours in Afghanistan, Mike decided to set up a program with members of other units; people he didn't know or serve with, but who were geographically within a 200-mile radius and willing to provide safe houses and vehicles for other members at a moment's notice with no questions asked through back channel communications. The agreement was to settle on any necessary repairs or costs associated with use of the property after danger had passed. It was a partnership he valued as much as his MAG group. While the MAG group was a close-knit group who lived close to one another and practiced drills in case of natural disaster or terrorist attack in their area, this partnership was strictly tied to individual emergencies most likely to be related to retaliation for activity in the military. Protocol was for each member to be willing to provide a vehicle to an assigned member with no warning and to be willing to provide shelter to another assigned member with warning. Mike had gone straight to Sam's with no warning, and Sam was to contact Aaron about the house so that no communication could be traced to Mike. There was no paperwork that tied Mike to Sam or Aaron, and they didn't socialize in public together. They kept their contact to a minimum and found discreet ways to communicate. Mike had been careful to find units who had never served on deployment near his or at the same time and to investigate each member thoroughly before asking them to join. It seemed a bit over-the-top to some of his team members who ultimately declined to participate, but to many in the service doing what he did, they felt it was better to be safe than sorry. This was the first time the connection had been used, and Mike was excited to see how it worked so he could offer improvements.

After being convinced the house was secure, Mike settled into watching security on the setup in the living room. It was different from his and certainly not as robust, but it would do. He saw the glimmer of the moon on the lake in the background as he focused his energy on over watch through the monitors.

Meanwhile, Kate was tossing and turning in the bed. It was softer than the bed at Mike's, but so were the pillows. She thought exhaustion would eventually wear her out, but it was difficult to turn her brain off, even for a couple of hours. She had failed to go to sleep before Jason, which meant she had to listen to his snoring before going to sleep. Finally, she drifted off with her head in an upright position against the headboard.

Norman appeared at 5 am to relieve Mike. Both were startled by Kate's sudden appearance in the living room. "You need to get some sleep," Mike said.

"Yeah, I'm trying. I just woke up with this terrible crick in my neck and a growling stomach. So now my mind is awake," Kate said as she rubbed the base of her skull and sat down next to Norman.

"I'm off to catch some Zs before we start tomorrow. Kate, check the kitchen if you want. I'm not sure what is in there, but help yourself," Mike said as he walked toward one of the bedrooms off the kitchen.

Kate still wondered about the connection of Mike to this house. It didn't seem his type at all, but he seemed familiar with the layout and comfortable in it. She was determined to figure that out after all this was over. She decided to take Mike up on the offer about the kitchen, even though it felt odd to eat some stranger's food without permission. She opened the freezer in hopes of a decadent treat and was delighted to find chocolate ice cream. She never let herself eat ice cream anymore; it was one of those foods that really offered her nothing in terms of nutrition and added to her already oversized hips. But it was comfort food, and she was in desperate need of comfort. She searched the cabinets and drawers for a bowl and spoon and started to dig out a helping. She offered Norman some, and he took her up on it.

She put the ice cream back into the freezer and started into the living room with both bowls. She sat on the couch with her feet under her and started to enjoy her ice cream. Norman kept one eye on the screens but turned to engage her in conversation. "So how are you holding up?" he asked.

"You know, I've been through just about every emotion I can think of this weekend, but I think I've finally gotten over the fear stage. I'm tired and frustrated, and more determined than ever to end this," Kate said, surprising herself. She took another bite of the ice cream.

"Good. I'd like to go home sometime soon," Norman said with a mouthful of ice cream. Norman was rough around the edges. He was a true redneck, but he had proven himself to be a good friend to have in a crisis. Kate suddenly realized what he must be giving up to be helping her.

Kate dropped the spoon back into the bowl. "Oh, Norman, I have been so self-absorbed that I hadn't even thought to ask how this was affecting you or Mike or the rest of the MAG group. I'm sure all you guys have much better things to do than to babysit me and my family. I really appreciate all that you've done. And I'm sorry I've dragged you into this. Especially since it seems to be rather dangerous."

"Are you kidding? Since I left the service 5 years ago, I haven't seen any action at all. I live for this stuff – the adrenaline is a rush. Don't get me wrong, a little of it goes a long way," Norman chucked. "This is what the MAG group is for, Kate. Otherwise, we are just a bunch of crazy conspiracy theorists prepping for the zombie apocalypse."

Kate laughed at his description, as that is exactly what she had thought of Jason's group before this weekend. She took another bite and asked, "You aren't a bunch of crazy conspiracy theorists prepping for the zombie apocalypse?"

"Oh yeah, we are. This just legitimizes our existence to nonbelievers like you," Norman teased.

Kate smiled, "So, what is up with the truck and the house? How are they not tied directly to Mike? And who was that guy Sam?"

"Ah, now see, crazy conspiracy theorists can't divulge secret connections to outsiders. Truth is, I'm not entirely sure, but I know Mike. And if he says it's secure, it's secure."

Kate was again frustrated with the lack of information. "You and Mike go way back?" Kate asked, fishing for information.

"A few years," Norman answered, again unwilling to give up much.

Kate rolled her eyes and grunted. "You guys are killing me!" She stirred what was left of the ice cream to make it soft and then finished it up. She noticed Norman was finished with his as well. She took both the bowls to the kitchen, washed, dried and retuned them to the cabinet before returning to the living room.

"I've never been in a situation like this before." Kate confessed.

"It shows, honey!" Norman joked.

Kate started to be defensive and then decided he was right. She should be grateful and not grumble. "Yeah, us regular women kind of stink at this sort of thing, huh?"

"I wouldn't say that. Well, maybe, but you don't seem much like a regular woman to me."

Kate was taken back by Norman's words. There was more underneath him that he didn't let show often. "How is that?" Kate asked, fishing for something to make her feel better about herself.

Norman wasn't one to get a gushy or give too many compliments. "You've done pretty well through this, all things considered. Don't let it get you down. I've seen enough action in my time to know that you just gotta push through. It will work out. We've got your back."

"Ok, I'm going to try to go back to sleep. Thanks, Norman - for all of this," Kate said quietly.

"Not a problem. Jason is a standup guy," Norman offered, "and you aren't too bad yourself."

Kate retreated to the bedroom. Jason had stopped snoring, and Kate was hopeful that she could sleep. She grabbed a towel from the bathroom and put it under her pillow for more support. She laid down and closed her eyes, finally drifting off to sleep.

Chapter 20

Kate snoozed lightly. Jason turned over in the bed, and his movement jarred her awake. She could tell from the light in the room under the white faux wood blinds that the sun was starting to rise. She decided to get up and head to the living room. She entered to see the sun glistening on the lake behind the house. Kate could see the edge of the lake was surrounded by houses, all with their own boat slips. "What lake is that?" Kate asked Norman.

"Allatoona."

"Oh, so we are in Acworth?"

"Yep," Norman answered. Kate was relieved to be close to home.

"Think it's ok if I make us some breakfast?" Kate asked.

"You better!" Norman joked.

Kate started looking in the refrigerator and cabinets for anything resembling breakfast items. She had heard Sam say whoever owned this house was on vacation so she wasn't holding her breath. She was delighted to find eggs and bacon. Once she saw some cheese, she decided breakfast sandwiches were the way to go. Kate hunted for bread but didn't see any in the bread box. Then she remembered seeing a loaf in the freezer last night. She pulled it out and started making the sandwiches. She hoped her secret house hosts were not health-conscious. Margarine didn't make the bread crusty like butter did. If there was one thing Jason did get worked up about, it was having to eat margarine, which he said was one molecule away from plastic. Jason had very distinctive tastes and habits. He was a gentlemanly redneck, if there was such a thing. His Southern drawl combined with his deep dimples and Matt Damon-esque smile that turned down first before up melted Kate's heart. But it was his chivalry that kept it. Jason had unusual hobbies – like the ham radio and his prepper group – but he was one of the good guys. He put up with Kate's quirkiness and worked hard to always edify her in whatever he did. And she loved him for that.

"Yay," Kate let out a small cry of joy.

"You ok in there?" Norman asked.

"Oh yeah, I just found some butter and was excited," Kate said.

"Butter? You are a strange lady," Norman said.

Kate started to explain and then stopped, "Um – it's a long story."

Kate started cooking and went to wake up Jason just before finishing. She found him sitting on the edge of the bed tying his shoes. "Is that bacon?" Jason asked gleefully.

"What else could it be?" Kate said.

"Um, mmmm, nothing like fried pig!" Jason said with a smile.

"Ok, 3 minutes until it's ready.

There wasn't any milk in the refrigerator, but she found some orange juice. She got everything ready and called the others to eat. They were delighted to have a hot meal, but all four of them were tired and worn out. The past 48 hours had taken its toll.

"Before we go to the Red Tiger, I want to see the boys," Kate said. Jason knew she was serious, and although he felt the same way, he wasn't too sure they should.

"I'm not sure Mike can make that happen," Jason agreed.

"I've been thinking about it all night. We can do a switch at the mall. Lots of people, lots of traffic. Brett can pick us up there and take us over to the house. We can do the drop at a different place in the mall on the way back. Mike, you said there is no connection to you, this property, or the truck on paper. How are they going to find us? We just need to make sure we aren't followed coming back and do some evasive maneuvers in the mall before they come get us," Kate offered.

"Evasive maneuvers?" Jason laughed. "I'm sure that will be so easy with your knee."

"It's better today. I have compression on it. You know what I mean anyway. We can do this. We have to do this."

Jason stared at her with a blank face. He wanted to see the boys, but it seemed risky.

"I have to see them, Jason. What if it's the last time? I need them to know I love them!"

"They know, Kate. Mike?" Jason asked.

Mike sighed and didn't answer.

"Norman, you can drop us off at the upper entrance to Macy's at 10:30 am. We can weave through the shop and come out at the food court at 10:45 am where Brett can pick us up. Then Brett can drop us at the movie theatre at noon. They'll be busy for the first matinee.

We can weave through the crowd and wander through the mall to the Footlocker entrance where Norman can pick us up at 12:15 pm," Kate offered her plan confidently.

"If they are watching the house, they are going to see us coming and going. It's a risk, Kate," Jason said.

"Only if Brett isn't good at spotting a tail," Kate protested.

"Oh, Brett knows how to spot a tail alright. I wouldn't worry about that. I'd worry more about them spotting you coming down the drive in his car or getting in and out of the house." Mike added.

"Then let him drive my dad's van. There's plenty of room to get on the floor in that thing. He can park in the garage, and we can enter unseen that way into the basement," Kate offered.

"Boys have confirmed all is quiet and no tails when they've been coming and going lately, Mike," Norman said.

"Ok, you win," Mike conceded. "I'll set it up."

Kate smiled. She was happy one of her crazy ideas seemed to be working out. "And then we'll go to the Red Tiger, right?"

"Right," Mike confirmed.

Chapter 21

Kate and Jason exited the truck at 10:30 at the upper entrance to Macy's. Jason held the door for Kate, as always, as they entered the building. Kate snickered to herself, thinking about the cloak and dagger she was about to engage in with her husband and then immediately felt sick. She had no idea what she was doing. She wondered if all those shows and movies she watched were based on some form of truth. She hoped so, as she was about to steal their moves.

Kate weaved in and out of the men's department at a reasonable pace, pretending to look at clothing for Jason while scoping for a tail. She zig-zagged to the mall entrance of the store, but instead of exiting, she made a loop and headed back the way they came. After realizing there wasn't anyone else in the men's department, Kate pulled Jason toward the escalator which led down to the main floor where they proceeded to the mall exit of the store. Kate pulled Jason through the mall with her arm wrapped through his, again pretending to look at shops as they passed, pointing her finger at different window displays. Jason thought it was a bit much and wasn't really interested in playing along.

"Come on, this is fun!" Kate said.

"Fun? I wouldn't ever call walking through the mall fun, but have you forgotten what is going on?" Jason asked.

"No, I'm just trying to not grumble and complain when bad things happen. It's new for me, so go with it. I'm shopping with my husband in the mall on the way to see my kids," Kate said, proud of her attitude. "And I'm pretending to be a spy losing a tail. Who would have thought I would ever get to be a spy!" Kate whispered happily.

Jason rolled his eyes. His wife was an unusual woman, that was for sure.

Kate spotted a toy store, dropped arms with Jason, and darted in. Jason followed and asked, "Hey, what are you doing?"

"I can't go empty handed. You have your wallet, right?" Kate asked.

"Yes, but we have to go, remember?" Jason said.

"I know. I'll just grab something quickly," Kate replied. Jason rolled his eyes. He wondered if this was necessary, but Kate was unaffected by his disinterest. She hurried through the aisles and found the Legos. There should be mini figures around here somewhere she thought. She scanned the shelves and came up empty. She tapped her fingernail on her front tooth as she thought for a second and then darted back to the cash register. "Ah ha!" she said as she found a Minecraft box with a mystery mini figure in it.

Jason was about 10 paces behind her. "I thought you didn't like that stuff, Kate," he reminded her.

"I don't. But we don't have much time. It's fine. They'll love it," Kate rationalized.

Kate held out her hand for Jason's wallet as the cashier rung them up. Fortunately, Jason had a $20 in his wallet. She didn't want to take any chances with a digital footprint. She had seen way too many shows where people get caught using credit cards. The cashier put the items in a bag, and Kate and Jason left the store, back on track.

"See, less than 2 minutes!" Kate bragged.

"I know, you are ruthlessly efficient," Jason teased.

"And you love that about me," Kate smirked.

"You just keep thinking that, and we'll be fine," Jason teased back. He tolerated her need for speed, but certainly didn't love that about her. He was confused about her behavior, but Kate was always acting strange. In some ways, her odd behavior was par for the course. Jason decided to enjoy it.

Once they approached the middle of the mall, Kate started toward the stairs. Jason stopped dead in his tracks and said, "Really? I don't think pretending you are a spy is actually going to make your knee not hurt."

Kate knew he was right. She switched directions, grabbed his hand, and headed for the elevator. The escalator was several hundred feet behind them, and she wasn't sure how much time they had. The elevator arrived quickly, but the door was slow to close. Kate immediately regretted her decision to choose the elevator over the longer walk to the escalator. She stiffened up, and prayed no one else would enter. An arm suddenly appeared through the center of the two doors just before it closed. A man dressed in black, 40s, entered the elevator quickly. He nodded his head to Jason and turned to face the doors as the elevator slowly creeped up to the next level. Kate's heart raced as she wondered if this was another goon. Hadn't she been careful in the mall? Maybe she wasn't that good. She noticed there was something under his jacket that might be a weapon. She could feel Jason's hand starting to sweat. Or was that hers? Relax, Kate, she told herself. The elevator was glass all the way around. If he was going to do something, everyone could see. She knew that was true, but she wondered if it would be too late anyway or if people at the mall ever even looked at the elevators. No, he could slash her throat and exit to get Chinese food, and no one would even notice. She closed her eyes and prayed hard for God to save them yet again.

The "level 2" light came on, and Kate heard the ding. The doors slowly started to open. The man rushed out and started jogging down the aisle. Kate watched carefully as they exited the elevator. The man bent down and picked up a little girl and hugged her. A lady with the girl leaned in to kiss him. She really has seen too many spy movies, Kate thought to herself.

Jason and Kate stood at the entrance to the food court just inside the vestibule until they spotted a white van. Jason pulled Kate toward the door, and they exited the building just in time to meet Brett at the curb. Jason pulled the door open for Kate and climbed in the front seat. Kate hit the automatic close button and sat in the captain's chair of the van.

"Thanks for picking us up. Any tails?" Jason asked

"No, all has been quiet. I left a while ago and looped around Acworth before heading this way. I circled back several times. No tails. We are clear, but that doesn't mean they aren't watching the house," Brett answered.

"Yeah, we are going to get in the floorboard when we approach," Jason said.

The ride to the house was quiet. Kate didn't know Brett well, and wasn't really in the mood for small talk. "How is my family?" Kate finally asked.

"The kids are fine; they think all of this is cool. The officers on duty have been showing them their equipment. Landon is especially taken with the backseat. I hope he doesn't get too comfortable in a squad car, if you know what I mean," Brett chuckled. "Your parents are more confused than anything. I haven't told them much, only that we were participating in a drill sponsored by local law enforcement. They don't know there is real danger, but you can tell your mom is concerned, especially about your absence. We've got 2 sets of uniforms on property today and 8 of us from the MAG team."

Kate wasn't sure what or how she was going to explain when she got there. She just needed to see the boys and hug them, just in case. They rode in silence toward the house. Kate was trying to formulate her words to not scare the boys or her parents. As they reached the road where they lived, Jason turned to Kate and said, "Do you need my help?"

"No, I can do it, but you'll have to go first" she grumbled back. Jason climbed toward the back of the van where the last row of seats had been tucked under in the stow-n-go holster. He laid down on the floor and offered his hand out to help Kate. She started to take it and realized it would be easier on her own. She stuck her hands out on the floor and rolled from the seat to the floorboard of the van just as the van took a curve. She lost her balance and groaned as her knee hit. Kate planted her face into the floor board of the van, frustrated.

"You ok?" Jason asked.

"Yeah," Kate said through the carpet, her head still smashed against it. "Just not a very graceful spy, I suppose."

"But a beautiful one," Jason said back with a smile.

Kate looked up at him. She knew it was lip service, but she liked it. "Yeah?" she teased. "So you think I should get a Black Widow outfit for our next op?"

"Forget the next op, get it just for me," Jason quipped back. He leaned in to kiss Kate as he pulled the blanket over them.

Chapter 22

Kate stayed perfectly still as the van entered the driveway. Brett slowed at their makeshift gated entrance halfway down the long driveway and waved at one of the MAG group patrollers. He pulled into the garage around the back of Kate's parents' house and closed the garage door. The windows of the door were already obscured, and Tommy had been stationed at the back of the house for watch. Brett opened the side door to the van and said, "All clear. I'll get everyone downstairs in the den."

Kate threw the blanket off and pushed herself to all fours. She put her forearm on the captain's chair and pulled herself up to a crouched position so she could exit the van. She grabbed onto the door to let herself down easily and waited for Jason. He hopped out behind her and put his hand in the small of her back as he led her into the house. There were no outside windows in the hallway from the garage to the den. As they entered the den, Kate dropped the bag of toys just inside the door. She noticed someone had already covered the very small windows in the den. She was excited to see the kids and felt safe with all the protection that had been provided.

"Momma! Momma!" Landon screamed as he bounced down the steps. Kate's heart was full. Tears filled her eyes, and she tried to push them back as Landon entered the room. He ran to her and jumped as she grabbed him and picked him up. Fortunately, he only weighed 45 pounds. Logan was on his heels.

"Momma!" Logan said softer with a big smile.

Jason sat on the couch and reached for Logan. "Daddy!" Logan shouted.

Kate's mom and dad entered the room. Her dad said with a smile, "Hey, you do exist! We thought you escaped and left the varmints with us."

"I know, Dad, I'm sorry – "Kate answered as Landon kissed her cheeks repeatedly. She put Landon down and reached down to hug Logan.

"Pick me up, Momma!" Logan said with a smile. Kate dreaded that; he was nearly 65 pounds. Instead, she leaned down and kissed him on the cheek, and he stepped back, wiping the kiss away. She still couldn't understand why he hated kisses so much.

Kate sat on the couch next to Jason and pulled Logan to her lap. Landon had made it to Jason's lap, but was jealous when Logan got to sit with Kate. Landon pushed Logan and climbed on top of her. Kate fell backward against the couch back and laughed. "Wait a minute! Wait a minute!"

"Boys! Get off your momma," Jason ordered.

"Momma, you HAVE to see the back of the police car! Mr. Springfield closed the door, and I couldn't get out!" Landon said.

"You couldn't?" Kate asked.

Logan talked over her, "And he turned the lights on. They are really bright at night!"

"So you are having fun with the police and Daddy's MAG group?" Kate asked.

"Yeah, but why didn't we go to church today," Logan asked.

Before Kate could answer, Landon interjected, "Can Sam come over and play? Please, Momma, please?"

"Yeah, yeah, yeah, can Sam come over?" Logan begged.

"Ok, listen, you, two," Kate started. Landon continued mouthing "please" and held his hands in a prayer position, inching closer to her face with every second. Jason reached his arm over and pulled Landon back gently and gave him a look. "Listen!" Kate repeated. Logan instantly fell in line, but Landon continued with his pleas.

"Landon!" Jason said loudly. Landon glared at his daddy and wrinkled his nose. Jason wanted to jerk him up and settle this, but he knew how important this was to Kate. He decided to let it play out a little before intervening.

"Mommie and Daddy have to do a few things, and then we'll be back. What do you think about having game night when we get back?" Kate offered.

"Where are you going? Can we go?" Landon asked enthusiastically.

"No, baby, not where we are going," Kate answered.

"No fair!" Landon whined. "Then Sam needs to come over."

"Life is not fair, Landon," Kate's dad interjected. It was phrase she always hated to hear when she was growing up, but she appreciated it more as an adult.

Landon pretended to not hear the words, "I'm going to call Sam, and he's going to come over." He turned his head away from Kate and folded his arms in a huff.

Kate was afraid her visit was about to get hijacked by an emotional outburst. She knew she couldn't let Sam come over, and certainly wouldn't have with the attitude Landon was displaying, but she needed this to be a good visit.

"Hey, you know what?" Kate asked. "I forgot. I have something for you!"

"You do? What is it? Is it a dog?" Logan asked.

"Well, it's super-secret," Kate answered hoping to draw Landon in. "I could tell you what it is, but then I'd have to kill you."

"Kill us?" Logan asked, confused. "Why would you kill us?"

Ok, so maybe that was over his head Kate thought. "Well, I can give it to you, but only if you promise to not show it to anyone outside this room."

Landon unfolded his arms and turned back to Kate. "Why not?" he asked.

"Because it's super-secret. If you show it to anyone, then THEY will want one, too." Kate said. She clearly wasn't very good at this, but it seemed to have taken Landon's attention from the whole Sam visit, at least for the moment.

"Well, they aren't getting mine!" Landon said loudly, laughing. He turned to his grandfather and said, "You can't have mine, Grandpa!"

Logan followed suit as always and said, "Yeah, Grandpa, you can't have mine."

Kate's mother played along and said, "What about me? Will you share with me?"

"Well, for a little while," Logan said.

"Ok, then, remember, it's super-secret. You have to keep up with it until I get back. Don't let anyone capture it. This is your responsibility until I get back, ok?" Kate said.

"OK!" both boys said almost in unison as Kate got up from the couch. She grabbed the bag from the floor and put the toys behind her back.

"Close your eyes and hold out your hands," Kate said.

The boys complied, and Kate put the toys in their hands. They opened their eyes and smiled. "Minecraft! Thank you, Momma!" Logan started.

"Yeah, thank you, Momma!" Landon said as he opened it.

The boys tore into the boxes and opened the figures, comparing the two and laughing. They instantly started
168

playing as if they had something secret and plotted their moves as they ran into the next room.

"Mom," Kate started, "I know this is all a little weird – "

"Yeah, you could say that," Kate's mom interrupted with a hint of sarcasm. She was a slender woman in her early 70s with white hair. She had taught kindergarten for years and was fantastic with her kids. She had a servant's heart and was always willing to do anything for anyone, especially Kate. Kate hated to always impose but seemed to never be able to stop herself. This weekend was an example of her dumping problems on her parents yet again, and for that, Kate felt horrible.

"I know, I know. And I'm sorry we didn't give you any warning about this weekend. We just didn't know what was involved," Kate tried to spin the events.

"Is this some sort of government thing? The police have been here since last night," Kate's dad asked. He was an interesting fellow with many quirks, but Kate revered him. Everything she learned about compassion, service and mercy came from her mom, but everything she learned about business, fairness, and never giving up came from her dad. He teased about the boys being a nuisance, but in truth, he loved them and couldn't see them enough. It had been his idea for Kate and Jason to build a house in front of theirs, sharing the property. He wanted to make an impression on his grandkids and help raise them his way. He was easily frustrated with the boys' antics, but he always welcomed them at his house.

"Kind of," Kate answered.

"Do you want some lunch? Let's go upstairs, and I'll fix some leftovers," Kate's mom said, always the servant.

"No, Mom, we have to go. We'll be back soon." Kate said.

"Are you in some sort of trouble?" Kate's dad asked. "What's with all the strange people hanging around and parking in the garage? Your friend made me move my Studebaker, which was no small feat." It might have seemed like a strange question, but Kate's dad was always working in the garage on a car; he didn't actually park in the garage with vehicles he drove.

She knew she needed to come clean, but her parents were not the kind of people who would understand all of this. She wasn't the kind of person who understood it all either. "I told you those guys are from Ken's MAG group. You know how weird they are," Kate said, hoping to get out of telling the whole truth. "I'm sorry you had to move your car. I'll help you push it back in when we get back."

"Yeah you will. It will take both you and Jason to help me get it back into place," Kate's dad gruffed.

 "And there's nothing for me to worry about?" Kate's mother asked again, clearly not buying Kate's excuse.

"It's a long story, but I promise I'll explain it to you when we get back. Can you watch the boys a couple more hours while we try to wrap things up?" Kate pleaded as she hugged her mother.

"Ok, if you are sure there isn't anything to be worried about," Kate's mom answered. "Will you call me if you need me?"

"Love you, Mom," Kate said, not wanting to address the lost phone again. She walked to the edge of the den. "Boys, come give me a hug. I have to go," she called out.

"Don't forget they have school tomorrow, Kate," her mom said.

Landon and Logan came running and grabbed her legs. "Bye, Momma!" they both said and ran back off to play with their new toys.

Kate was satisfied with the visit. She and Jason walked back down the hall and exited into the garage. They closed the door behind them so her parents wouldn't notice them getting under the blanket on the floorboard. They climbed in the van and got back into position.

Getting back into the seat was as challenging as getting out of it had been, but Kate managed. She rode in silence on the way back to the mall, wondering if her parents picked up on her anxiousness. Kate prayed once again, asking God to protect them on this mission, to help them resolve the issue and do the right thing so that she could go back to being a normal person again with her family.

The van stopped in front of the box office entrance to the mall. Kate was right; the theater was busy with the first matinee, and there was a crowd. She and Jason weaved through the crowd, careful to look behind them for followers. Kate turned right at the fork in the mall traffic, opposite of the way to the Footlocker entrance. Jason started to question her and decided it was best just to let her do her thing.

The two walked quicker through the mall this time than before. Kate entered a couple of stores and made quick loops to check her six. She didn't see anyone following, but she wasn't sure. This was the dangerous part. The bad guys had found her at Mike's. If they were watching the house and followed the van, they could easily pick her up and follow her back to their new safe house. As a red head, Kate was very descriptive. She was easy to spot in a crowd and because of her size, she didn't think changing her hair color would make much of a difference to hide her identity. She opted to just be on the lookout as they weaved from store to store. She turned back toward stores she had been into and circled them again. Finally, she made her way to Footlocker. As they rounded the corner, Jason saw the black Dodge Ram approach the entrance. He grabbed Kate's hand and pulled her quickly to the doors. They climbed into the back seat of the truck, and Norman exited the mall with Mike in the front seat.

"Any trouble?" Mike asked.

"No," Kate answered.

"We didn't see anyone tailing us, but it would be better if you guys watched out for us," Jason said.

"We are going to drive through the square and around the loop before heading to the restaurant. If there is a tail, we'll see them," Mike said confidently.

Chapter 23

The drive seemed to take forever, but Kate was happy Mike was being cautious. Finally, the Dodge Ram pulled into the parking lot of the Red Tiger, next to Xdrenaline.

Norman parked in a spot easy to get out. The four of them exited the vehicle and started for the door. Kate grabbed Jason's hand and squeezed. She wasn't sure what they were going to find. The restaurant was busy with the after-church lunch crowd. Kate knew the crowd offered cover – part of why the incident at Sunny's happened was because there were no witnesses. Norman went in first, just in case. Jason held the door for Kate as he always did and released it to Mike who brought up the rear. This formation seemed to be the safest, so Kate wasn't interested in changing it. Everything looked normal. Kate walked up to the counter. She took a deep breath while the cashier finished her paperwork from the last customer. She showed the girl behind the counter the email with the free offer from Norman's phone, and asked, "Do you honor this offer?"

"What you order?" She asked with a heavy Chinese accent.

Kate was confused. "No, I want to know if you honor this offer?" she asked.

"What you order?" She asked again, clearly frustrated with Kate.

"Um, sweet and sour chicken, I guess," Kate answered.

"You want white or flied lice?"

"White, please," Kate answered.

"You want drink?"

"Sweet tea, please."

The girl looked up at Jason. "What you order?"

"Oh, I'm with her," Jason said.

"You order. You eat. Then I honor offer. You Americans always in hurry."

"Oh, ok. Chicken fried rice, an egg roll, and a Coke" Jason answered.

"And you two? What you order?" the girl asked Mike and Norman

"Two kung pow chickens and two sweet teas," Norman answered.

"$34.42."

Kate handed the girl two $20 bills.

"You sit. I bring out." The girl instructed as she passed Kate her change.

Kate turned around and glared at Jason with her eyes wide open as if to say, "What just happened?"

Jason leaned in and hummed the theme to "The Twilight Zone".

Mike wanted the booth in the corner where he could see the entire restaurant, but he'd have to settle for the table next to it since the booth was occupied by a family that didn't look as if they were leaving anytime soon. The four of them sat, anxiously awaiting the food so they could get whatever gift they were supposed to get.

"You packin'?" Mike asked Jason quietly.

"Always," Jason answered, much to Kate's displeasure. She was uncomfortable with guns, but Jason had always wanted her to carry. She imagined that someone would take the gun from her before she could use it. Ever since she was a little girl, Kate wanted to be a detective, but she had settled for investigator all those years ago because there was no weapon requirement.

"Just be ready in case this goes sideways," Mike warned.

"Copy that," Norman and Jason agreed.

The food arrived without incident, and the four of them ate quickly. Kate nearly choked hers down. She was nervous and unsure what was going on. The server on the floor refreshing drinks had been by twice. Eventually she cleared half the plates at the table. Kate was starting to wonder if they really were going to get this gift or if the emails were a hoax, or worse, a dead end. An elderly woman appeared from behind the curtain blocking the kitchen. She approached the table with her hands clasped. Kate took a deep breath and gripped the chair. If she had to move quickly, she was going to need the chair's support to make an escape.

The woman bowed and offered her hands out in front of Kate, revealing a fortune cookie.

"Inside this fortune are answers you seek. Be careful; danger comes when we know too much about our own fortune." The woman stared into Kate's eyes and paused awkwardly. Kate reached for the fortune cookie and took it from the woman. "Now you go. I have customer to serve," the woman ordered waving her hands at the group. "Here is take-out menu for next time," she said, shoving a menu in Kate's hand and squeezing tightly as she stared at Kate again.

Kate got the message that the menu was important and unfolded the it as the four of them exited the building in the same formation as always. There was a note in the upper right hand corner, "Sorry for the runaround. Needed time to exit agency. M" Kate showed the note to Jason as they entered the truck.

"This must be the end of the cat and mouse games, thank goodness."

"I wonder who 'M' is," Kate said.

"Who cares! What's in that fortune cookie?" Norman asked.

Kate opened the fortune cookie as the truck left the parking lot and headed back to base. She cracked the cookie open to reveal the fortune. "Badge, agency, acct, case, trans, routing" Kate read off. She wrinkled her nose and turned the fortune over. "Hmmm, that's interesting. The back has numbers on it like a regular fortune cookie– 3-14-26-11-15-20." Kate studied it some more. "These must be the excel sheet headers: Badge number, agency, account number, case number, transaction number, routing number," Kate screamed with excitement.

"What are the numbers for?" Norman asked.

"Nothing, or maybe the columns they match up to," Jason said. "But there are more columns in that sheet than six."

Jason frowned. "But this is the last clue. What do all those other columns mean?"

"Let's focus on the ones we do know. What do they mean?" Mike asked back.

Silence fell in the truck. Finally, Jason said, "Well, if we have an account and bank to and from, then it's a record of transferring of money, right? There are dates and dollar amounts in the file. Now we know the when, what, and how. We just need the why. Let me pull up the file."

Kate leaned over to see. "Does the badge column have four digits?"

"Yes," Jason answered. More silence.

Kate's mind was racing. Suddenly, she shouted, "It's a bribe to pay off the investigator to throw the clearance!"

"What?" Mike asked. "What clearance?"

"That's what kind of investigator I was. We did security clearances for government positions. If the file is recording money transactions with links to a badge number, then I bet this file is recording the bribe. A federal agency must be the sponsor. The badge number is the investigator. There's a date, amount, the routing number and account number of the bank – I bet that is where the money is coming from. Trans must be the transaction number, so you can find where the money went. The rest is like everything else – extra data to throw us off the trail."

"If you are right, this is big, Kate. We are in over our heads," Jason warned.

"It's definitely something someone would kill to protect. I understand why 'M' wanted to break it up," Mike said.

"But there aren't any letters in that file. How is the agency identified by numbers?" Norman asked.

"Probably by numeric code with the alphabet, like A=1, B=2, etc." Kate answered.

Jason looked at the file. "Well it's not the easy answer. Using A=1 doesn't seem to make sense."

Mike opened the glove compartment and searched for a pen or pencil. He handed Kate a blue pen and said, "See what you can figure out, Kate."

Kate wasn't sure she had the right skills to decrypt the file. She tried reversing the easy answer and making A=26. That didn't seem to work. She tried shifting it one number to A=2, B= 3, etc. That didn't work. Kate was easily frustrated by the challenge and let out a loud, "Grrr!"

"Just breathe, Kate," Mike said. "It'll come."

Kate stared at the paper for the next couple of minutes, scribbled different combinations down that didn't seem to work. She looked at the menu again and scribbled more on the paper. "It's in the note! It's in the note! M=1! That's it!" Kate shouted with glee. She leaned over to Jason, pleased with her find. "See, this one is BOP – Bureau of Prisons. This one is NSA. This one is DEA. This one is FBI," Kate said as she moved her pencil down the list she had decoded.

"We need to go to our FBI friend's house, now!" She knew it would be safer to go to the FBI office, but then she might be involved in a trial, or worse. Witness protection was not an idea that was pleasant to her. No, the best thing for her was to keep her name out of this and hand off the file to someone who knew what it was and what to do with it. Going to Schaeffer privately was her only hope of getting back to her normal life. Schaeffer had proved on two occasions that he would not hurt her, but that he was interested in the file. Kate wasn't sure he was completely innocent in all this, but he would have to do.

Norman almost ran off the road. "Are you crazy?" he asked. "He could be the one ready to kill for it. We can't just waltz up to his house. We need to wait until tomorrow and go to his office where there are a lot of FBI agents around."

"You said you didn't think he was dangerous, remember? We talked about this earlier, and you were on board," Kate said sarcastically.

180

"To his office. I was on board with going to his office. Plus, that psycho Kung Fu woman creeped me out with her fortune talk," Norman shouted back.

"That's why we have to get it to him now," Kate answered.

"She's right. The longer we have this file, the longer are at risk," Mike said.

Jason chimed in, "Yeah, who knows what side Kung Fu woman is on and who she will tell that we have the 'secret decoder ring'."

Kate thought about all the idiotic moves most women make in television shows she loved. Was this one of them? Would he sell her out? Did he send those guys to kill them? Even if he did, he had already shown he was unwilling to kill for it.

"If he wants us D-E-D dead, experience tell us it's going to be after we give up the file," Kate said.

"Oh, great, so he'll just kidnap and torture us until he gets the file. Yeah that's much better," Jason snapped in his best Alec Hardison (from *Leverage*) voice to match Kate's quote from the same character about 'D-E-D'.

"What if he is in on it?" Norman asked. "If the FBI is on the list, he could be the one arranging the bribes. He could have killed Scott Brown. You said it was weird Scott hadn't given the file to Schaeffer yet. Sounds to me like he didn't trust him."

"Maybe, but why hasn't he killed us?" Kate asked.

"Fair point. Maybe he doesn't know for sure we have the file," Jason said.

"Well, we have it now, and we have to do something with it or this won't end. If the FBI is bribing investigators then it will go all the way to the top, not just be at some low-level field agent," Kate said.

"You are right about that. And if the head of the FBI was after the file and knew we had it, Schaeffer wouldn't have soft pedaled it so much with us," Mike said. "What do you want to do, Kate?"

Kate thought for a minute. She took a deep breath and prayed out loud, "Lord give us wisdom. You've brought us this far, and I trust you will see us through. I need to be there for my children, Lord. You know how precious they are. Thank you for your blessings on us, for keeping us safe, for providing me with Jason, Norman and Mike to protect me the past few days, for the loving support of a wonderful husband. Give me the strength to do what has to be done and the wisdom to know what that is. In Jesus' holy name, I ask these things." At least two minutes passed before a wave of peace came over Kate.

"Are you with me?" she asked Jason.

He grabbed her hand and said, "I promised until death do us part. I'll let you know if I change my mind."

Kate enjoyed his humor and appreciated his support. She had truly been blessed by a loving husband who would go to the ends of the earth with her. Literally.

"You guys have my back?" she asked Norman and Mike.

"You know it," Mike answered.

Ok, let's go to his house. 1725 Fallsbrook Circle." Kate announced. "It's in Brookstone, right down the street from our house."

Norman turned the truck around and headed that direction. "We'll have to drive around a little before we find it. Mike, we need a plan of attack."

"I have a plan," Kate announced.

"Attack!" Jason quickly interjected, finishing the line from *The Avengers* with a smirk.

Kate laughed, but Norman and Mike didn't get the joke. That was nothing new. Jason and Kate seemed to have their own inside jokes with quoting television and movies that few others understood. "No, seriously, I do. I'm going to make a trade with him. He wants the file. I want my life back," Kate said boldly.

"You are just going to walk up to his house and ask him to trade?" Norman chided.

"Yep. Sure am. You guys will have my back, but you are the ones that convinced me his is not dangerous. If he really wants the file, then he'll hear me out."

"This isn't one of your television shows, Kate. He has a huge home turf advantage, and we don't know what side he's on. What makes you think he won't try something?" Mike asked.

"Because we have the surprise advantage. He won't expect us to come to his house," Kate said. "He might have some firepower, but he's not going to shoot us in front of his family on a Sunday afternoon in his living room."

"Ok, we'll play it your way, but if we sense danger, I'm pulling the plug quickly before it gets out of hand," Mike said.

"Fair enough," Kate answered. "Norman, head down Mars Hill to Brookstone. If you turn right into the subdivision, we can find it." Kate turned her attention back to the file and Jason. "Can you put the headers in and change the agency codes to the letters so the file is complete?"

"You know I can," Jason said as he started typing away.

Chapter 24

Norman pulled into the subdivision and started looking for the street. "Fallsbrook Drive, Fallsbrook Terrace. Where is Fallsbrook Circle?"

"It's around here somewhere," Kate answered.

"There!" Jason shouted.

The road was short and had a cul-de-sac, not lending itself to a lot of reconnaissance without notice. Norman turned the truck and around and decided to park across the street on Fallsbrook Terrace. The four exited the vehicle. Kate could feel her heart racing yet again as she started walking toward the street.

"Whoa! Let's just take a minute and get ready," Mike said, pulling Kate's arm. Mike opened the cover on the bed of the truck and strapped on his leg holster. He handed Norman one as well. They moved their guns to the holsters for easier access. Both Mike and Norman put on their Kevlar vests and handed one to Jason.

"What about Kate?" Jason asked.

"I don't have one – " Mike stopped his sentence short.

"That will fit me?" Kate finished his sentence, irritated at herself. "Yeah, I know. Look, I'm good. He's not going to shoot me until he has that file." At least she hoped he wouldn't.

"Kate, these are really tight anyway. It barely goes around me, but I can cut this one into pieces for you," Jason said. "I'd feel better if you had something on in case things go South."

"Look, I don't want to freak this guy out too much. A show of strength is good so he doesn't bully me, but I don't think he's going to do anything to me. I really don't," Kate protested. "Let's just go and get this over with."

"Let's go steal ourselves an FBI agent," Jason whispered to Kate with a smile. Kate smiled back. Jason knew the reference to *Leverage* would help calm Kate a little, or at least through her anxiety off a little.

Mike and Norman checked their pockets and made sure all their gear was ready to go. The three of them put jackets over the vests to not stand out to the neighbors as much. There wasn't a way to conceal their weapons, and Mike was ok with that. He wanted this guy to know they meant business. "Let's move," Mike ordered as he started across the street.

Kate felt sick again. Was she really going to threaten an FBI agent? Yes, she was. She needed her life back, and John Schaffer was going to get it back for her.

Kate rang the doorbell and waited, citing Matthew 10:28 in her head. Do not be afraid of those who kill the body but cannot kill the soul. She took a deep breath as the door opened. A woman opened the door. She was the blonde from the photo. Her hair and makeup were perfect. She wore a colorful maxi dress with 5" stiletto heels. The silver necklace matched her earrings. "May I help you?" she asked.

"We are here to see John, please. It's important." Kate said.

The woman looked at the men with Kate. She gasped slightly and closed the door quickly, retreating into the house yelling, "John!"

Kate was suddenly feeling as if she had made a mistake. What if he came to the door with a gun and just shot them? She looked at Jason and squeezed his hand. He patted hers with his other hand and gave her a reassuring nod. The door opened, and John appeared. He was clearly as shocked to see her as she was afraid of him. "You?" he exclaimed.

"Yeah, me." Kate stood up straight and took a breath. "I have something you want, and you have something I want. We are going to make a trade." Kate said boldly in the sassiest voice she could muster. She couldn't believe the words came out of her mouth that easily.

"Ok, what do you want?" John asked.

"No, first I come in. Then we talk." Kate said. It was as if his surprise gave her confidence to be braver than she thought possible.

"Ok, just you, though. Your posse stays here," John said as he glared at Norman.

"No, these guys are with me. They come in, or I walk." Kate replied, knowing she held all the cards.

"Ok, fine. Come in," John said, holding the door for the four of them to enter. "Mandy, we are going to be in the study," he hollered down the hall and showed them into a small room off the back of the house.

Kate and "her posse" walked down the hall to the study where John led them. Kate was mildly concerned that John would try something. But his wife was in the house, so she thought they might be safe. Still, she was glad to have the protection with her.

"What is it that I can do for you, Ms. O'Connor?" John asked.

"I have the file you are looking for, but I want to know how you are involved in this and why before I give you anything," Kate said.

"I thought you said you didn't know what file I was talking about." John responded.

"Well, I do now." Kate answered, conjuring her best white trash voice once again.

"You have a recording device?" John asked.

"No, this is just between us," Kate said.

"How can I be sure you are telling the truth?"

"You can't. But I'm here to trade, not rat you out," Kate said.

"And how do I know you will give me the file if I tell you what I know?" John asked.

"You don't," Kate replied, calling his bluff. The two stared at each other intensely. After several seconds, Mike and Norman got up from their chairs as if to leave.

"Ok, Ms. O'Connor, you win. I'll tell you my side. And then you'll produce the file," John stated rather matter-of-factly.

Kate motioned to Mike and Norman to come back and sit. "Deal. Spill it." Kate ordered.

"Scott called Thursday right before lunch. He was sitting outside my office staring at me – it was kind of odd behavior. He said he was about to get something big and that I would be sorry I didn't help him all those years ago. Scott was always coming up with crazy schemes and conspiracy theories, none of which ever panned out. His voice was shaking and slow. I thought he was on drugs or something. I told him to come and show me, that we could talk it through. If he had something worthwhile, I'd see what I could do. He refused – said he just wanted me to know before he got the big win because he was going to do it in my town, right under my nose. Said he had someone he trusted outside the system that would do the right thing and not try to steal the credit like I would. I thought it was odd he wouldn't come in, so my partner and I followed him. We saw him give you the paper and figured you were the someone he could trust. I started to approach him, but he limped into the woods and disappeared. That was the last time I saw him alive."

"And that's your story?" Norman asked. "Sounds kind of shady to me. How do we know you didn't kill him?"

"Because we have the guy that did in custody," John said.

"Who? How did they figure it out so fast?" Kate asked.

"It isn't rocket science. Just good detective work," John condescended.

"You'll have to forgive me if I am a little hesitant to take your word for it. How do you know the man you have is Scott's killer?" Kate asked again, this time more sternly.

"Eye witness came forward about a stabbing at Waffle House after Scott's body was found," John started. "We got lucky with traffic cams that were just installed and were able to identify the man clearly once my team took over the investigation from the locals."

"Convenient, if you ask me," Norman said. "And how do you know all this since the FBI doesn't investigate local murders?"

Kate raised her hand to signal for Norman to let it go. "Why did he kill Scott?"

"He's a middle man. Cobb police are working the interrogation. He'll crack soon, but I can't comment anymore on an active investigation," John said, clearly hiding behind the badge.

"Ok, fine. Why did Scott leave the FBI?" Kate asked.

"One of his conspiracy theories went wrong. He claims he had a smoking gun but was told to stand down, and the case was closed."

"Did he have a smoking gun?" Kate pressed.

"I have no idea," John answered.

"Then why did he say you would be sorry?" Norman asked.

"Because I wouldn't help him try to get the case reopened. I had too much riding on my career to go chasing some ghosts, and Scott was angry with me about that," John answered.

"Ok, but how did you find me?" Kate asked.

John continued, "My partner followed you home from the school. We couldn't approach you like a normal investigation, as it wasn't sanctioned, and we didn't really know what was going on. I wasn't going to scare your family, and I couldn't risk being caught chasing ghosts again, especially off-book. But Scott was acting strange, and if he really had something big, I needed it. My career has stalled, and I keep getting passed over for promotions."

Norman punched Mike on the arm and smiled. He mimed playing a fiddle to show his sarcastic sympathy.

"And awards?" Jason added.

John shot him a look that could kill. "How do you know about that?" he asked.

"We can't comment on an active investigation," Norman jeered.

"It isn't rocket science; just good detective work," Jason added with a smile.

"Ok, guys," Kate said to the three of them to signal them to stop, even though she was enjoying the roasting after what Schaeffer had put them through over the past couple of days. She turned back to John and said, "I'm pretty handy with research, and your wife is pretty loose-lipped about your job online. She really should make her Facebook profile private. Now, continue, please."

"My partner swept your place the next morning while I followed you to work. I just wanted to talk to you, but you tried to punch me."

"Why didn't you just ask me like a normal person?" Kate asked, not impressed with his explanation. "Grabbing me in the parking lot wasn't your finest hour as an agent."

"Maybe not. But I didn't anticipate you being so violent. I was just trying to talk to you," John argued.

"Just trying to talk to me? You grabbed my hand and scared the life out of me!" Kate argued. "You are lucky I'm not a gun-toting member of the NRA like these guys," Kate snapped, pointing to her husband, Norman and Mike.

"Yeah, sorry about that. Guess I'm used to man-handling suspects who don't cooperate. I got a nasty bump on my head as punishment, though."

Kate smiled. Jason sat up straight with pride in his wife. "You went all female Jack Bauer on him, Babe."

Kate smiled back. She was proud of herself for not being a victim, even if he was just trying to talk to her. "But you searched my house? Without a warrant? Do you know the trouble you could be in if I pressed charges?"

"I didn't search your house," John said, pleased with himself on a technicality.

"No, you sent your partner to do your dirty work for you." Mike interjected.

"It's not like we took anything," John argued. "If you really have this file then you know how dangerous this game is. And if you are here, then you know I can help. I doubt you are going to get hung up on a little search that you can't prove happened."

"Just keep going," Kate ordered. She was angry about the invasion of privacy and knew Jason wouldn't be happy if she let it go, but John was right. There were bigger fish to fry here.

"After your house came up empty, and you went to the police, it was obvious that either Scott didn't pass anything to you or you didn't know what you had," John continued.

"How did you know about the police?" Jason asked.

"I have been doing this a while, ya know? And I'm the FBI. Local law enforcement in small towns will show me anything."

"Power trip much?" Norman asked.

John shot him a look and continued, "I concluded Kate was just a regular citizen, and the whole thing was just another of Scott's empty conspiracy theories. Until he showed up dead. That's when I realized it wasn't nothing."

"How do we know you aren't part of this whole thing? How can we be sure you aren't trying to save yourself from whatever is in that file?" Jason asked.

"If I was trying to protect myself, you wouldn't be standing in my study, 40 feet from my family." John said.

"You put the red flag on Scott's file?" Mike interrupted.

"Yeah, I was looking for any lead I could find to not only to help solve his murder but to link to whatever conspiracy he had uncovered," John answered.

"You tried to attack me again at Sunny's. How did you know I was there?" Kate asked.

"I had cleared you off the list and was working another angle. It was sheer luck that I was at Fort Benning on official business when the red flag came in. I had no idea it was you until we saw you in the restaurant."

"But you didn't just want to talk to me that time. You sent your goons out to attack us. Why?" Kate said.

"Experience, honey. We just went over last time I tried to talk to you," John reminded Kate.

"Oh yeah," Kate smiled and looked down. Jason winked at her and smiled. "So who was your posse that day?"

"Trainees," John answered. "They are hungry to do anything to impress a senior field agent."

"Why did you let us go?" Norman asked.

John turned his attention to Kate. "You are sassy. You gave quite a performance, and once I saw you had backup, well, I figured you were going to blow the whistle on me any minute for the parking lot incident. I had convinced the trainees you were an informant refusing to cooperate in an investigation. At some point, too many questions were going to be asked, and it still didn't seem you knew what you had, if anything --"

"So, you backed off," Jason finished John's thought.

"Yeah, he did." Norman chided as he reached out his hand to high-five Mike.

"Let's just say we went another route," John answered.

"Like sending the losers from last night?" Norman asked.

"What do you mean?" John asked.

Norman held his hands up to do air quotes, "The 'hitmen' you sent to Mike's house – Thomas Malcom and Frank Crenshaw. We almost bagged and tagged those guys," Norman bragged. "Lucky for them we left them for the sheriff to deal with."

"What? No, no, no, no!" John insisted. "All I did was I asked permission to make it official and use resources to actively investigate Scott's murder in cooperation with the police so we could uncover any conspiracy he had found."

"So you didn't follow us to Mike's place?" Kate asked.

"Mike? Who's Mike?" John asked.

Mike nodded at John, "That'd be me."

"No, I didn't follow you to his place," John answered. "Like you said, I backed off. I was working another angle."

"Then why did two guys show up at Mike's house with guns and then ask for the DEA to bail them out of jail?" Kate asked.

"I have no idea. If I were guessing, I'd say the file has something to do with the DEA. You don't know what's in the file?" John asked.

Kate tried to change the conversation back to her control. She knew what was in the file but wasn't ready yet to show her hand. "What have you found out about Scott's murder?"

"Strangely enough, it leads back to you," John said as he pointed to Kate.

"Me?" Kate asked, shocked at the comment. "How does it lead back to me?"

"Scott had been following you. Did you know him?" John asked.

"Yeah, but I didn't recognize him. It was nearly 12 years ago. He was my instructor at the Mine." Kate responded. "He was following me? Why?"

"You must have made quite an impression on him," John said with a smile.

"She was top in her class, as always," Jason bragged.

"Well, whatever it was, Scott must have thought you were the one to be trusted with this information," John said, "and the fact that you are here with it proves him right."

"I didn't say I brought it with me," Kate snapped and looked at Jason. "Why didn't he tell me what it was when he passed it to me? I had no idea it was some secret spy file. It was a fluke I even found the file from a flyer to a trampoline place."

Jason jumped in, "Because he knew you, Kate. You never give up on anything, and I bet he knew you wouldn't give up on that coupon until you figured out why it didn't work and found the right site and then followed this through."

"And because he was running out of time. According to the coroner's report, he had already been stabbed when he gave that paper to you. He probably didn't have enough strength to do much more but knew he had to pass the file off," John offered. "He died shortly after your encounter in the parking lot."

"He probably didn't even know all the steps he'd have to go through when he handed it to you. The apology about the runaround sounds like Scott wasn't ready for that and thought he was getting the whole file at once. My guess is Scott's original plan was to retrieve the file and then approach you to get it in the open. He didn't anticipate getting stabbed and having to move up his timeline." Mike noted.

"That was a pretty big risk he took," Kate said.

"Not if I know Scott," John answered. "He had crazy conspiracy ideas, but he was a great judge of character. I'm sure he knew you'd see it through, and he probably thought the less he said the harder you'd dig at it giving his file the best chance to be discovered."

"Well, he was right about that," Jason laughed. Kate wanted to protest, but she knew all too well her need to figure things out. It was true that anything that seemed like a mystery ate at Kate until she solved it.

"How do we know you will get the file to the right person?" Mike asked.

"You don't," John answered back in a tongue-and-cheek.

Well, played, Kate thought. She knew she had to honor Scott's life by finishing this, but she wasn't sure if John was trustworthy or not. "John, I need your word that you will get this to the right person and leave us out of it. We just want our lives back."

"You haven't even told me what the file is," John reminded them.

"Your word first," Kate ordered.

John hesitated, and Norman jumped on the opportunity. "You're not really going to give the file to him, are you? Kate, he broke into your hose. Scott didn't trust him with it - thought he'd use it for his own gain. Sounds like he had that about right," Norman protested.

"Yeah, and that's what I'm counting on," Kate said. "Scott's concern with keeping it from John was to make sure he received the credit for uncovering the conspiracy. We don't need the credit. What we need is for the truth come out. For us to be safe, we need to be as far away from this as possible. John will get it out in the open and expose the conspiracy because it benefits him. We've already seen what he's willing to do to boost his career."

"She's got a point, Norman," Mike interjected.

"John, the file contains details about bribes to OPM investigators. That enough information for you?" Kate asked.

"For clearance investigations?" John asked in disbelief. Kate shook her head in agreement. "How many are we talking?"

"Enough that it got Scott killed," Kate replied.

"Fair enough. I will get it to the right people. You have my word," John said.

"We think whoever has badge #1257 is the linchpin." Kate said.

"What makes you think that?" John asked.

"Well, it's kind of a long story, but it was in the first email I received." Kate answered.

"Email? I thought Scott gave you the file at the school?" John asked, puzzled at the response.

"He gave me the flyer I told you about in the parking lot. I wasn't lying about that," Kate said. "Made the performance easier to be telling the truth. I really didn't have the file until about an hour ago. It was given to us in three different pieces. We had to figure out and collect each piece of the puzzle to complete the file," Kate said.

"Well, I guess Scott had the right source after all," John commended Kate.

"I guess," Kate graciously accepted the compliment, still not sure she was deserving. The she turned serious once more, "Scott gets credit in the newspapers along with you for the discovery. You can spin it however you want to make sure you get the limelight and kudos for the find, but you let them know that Scott died trying to get this information out, and you leave me out of it or sass will be the least of your worries from me." Mike and Norman moved toward John, denying him of his personal space to back Kate's claim up.

"Understood," John agreed. "As long as the file checks out."

Norman and Mike backed up to a reasonable distance. Jason pulled the ipad out of the backpack and handed it to Kate. He pulled back, looked at John and said, "I want assurances my family will be left alone – that you will personally protect us, and not just for a couple of months. I mean you are our FBI agent on call for the foreseeable future. If we need anything, you handle it personally."

"If this is what you say it is, I'd be honored," John said eagerly. "And you will forget about our run-ins?"

"What run-ins?" Kate said with a smile. "A trade, like I said."

"Who were those goons from last night, John?" Jason asked. "The sheriff said they were connected to the DEA. My guess is someone on that list of bribes works for the DEA."

"Makes sense," John said. "I'll take care of them. You have my word on that."

Kate opened the ipad and pulled up the file. John couldn't believe his eyes. "Do you realize how damaging this could be to our entire country? I have to get this to the Director right away," he said in horror, moving toward the door.

"Is he trustworthy?" Kate asked, hoping she had made the right call.

"Yeah. I'd bet my life on it," John said.

"Good because you kind of are," Mike interjected.

"I'm going to need this ipad back, ya know?" Kate smirked.

"I'll buy you a new one," John answered with a chuckle. John pulled out his phone and punched in some numbers. "Tony, who's on rotation tonight?" John asked and paused for the answer. "Ok, send Jones and Slater to my house now. I've got an overnight for them. I'll fill you in when I get there. On my way once they arrive." John hung up the phone and looked at Jason. "Jones and Slater will take you to your house and set up a perimeter and protection detail for your family until we get this all wrapped up. Don't worry; I've got you covered."

Kate smiled and thanked John. They waited until the black SUV arrived at John's house before exiting. John went out to bring the agents up to speed and bark orders. "All clear, Kate," John shouted. As she exited the house, Kate felt empowered and exhausted all at the same time. She was overwhelmed when she thought the file had come to her randomly, but now to realize Scott did seek her out was more than she could process. She wasn't sure if she was flattered that he remembered her after all those years and trusted her with something so big or angry that he didn't consider the consequences to her life when he handed her that flyer.

Chapter 25

Kate and Jason had the FBI agents take them to the church to retrieve their cars. Kate wondered how she was going to explain all this to her parents. Jason dug the keys out of the backpack, opened her doors, and looked in her hatch. "Water, towels, my rifle, you really did prepare, didn't you?" he said, impressed with Kate's thought process.

"I grabbed what I could find, but then we had to leave it here, so I guess I didn't do such a good job after all," Kate replied, opening the car door.

"You did fine. It all worked out," Jason said as he tossed her the keys. Kate caught them, but then dropped them beside her door. As she bent down to get them, she saw the reflection of her phone shining under her seat. She thought about how different the first couple of hours might have been had she found her phone.

"I'm dying to go get the kids," Kate said, holding up the phone.

"Me, too," Jason agreed, "Hey, you found your phone."

"And not a minute too soon, either."

"Not a minute too soon? It's kind of after the time you needed it, isn't it?"

"Nah, if I had found the phone earlier, I would have called you instead of meeting you here." Kate smiled and paused for Jason to figure it out.

Jason thought for a minute. "And we wouldn't have figured out who Schaeffer was."

"Exactly. And this would have ended in a much different way, probably with me working at a gas station in our new Witness Protection life. Funny how God has a way of working things out for the good of those who love Him, huh?"

"You bet," Jason agreed. "How are you going to explain this to your parents?"

"I have no idea. I guess I'll just start at the beginning," Kate said.

"Can't think of a better place than that," Jason said as he got into his car.

Chapter 26

Kate curled up on the couch with Landon and Logan and turned on *How to Train Your Dragon*. The boys were wiggly, and she was surprised they all fit in the chair together. She had grabbed an old comforter so that they would each have plenty of cover and planned to enjoy snuggling with her kids before they were too big to enjoy it.

Jason brought the new ipad over to her. "Hey, check this out," he said with a smile.

Kate took the ipad and read the headline: Slain OPM Investigator, FBI Agent Uncover Huge Conspiracy.

"Momma, the movie!" Landon begged.

"I see it, Landon," Kate answered with a kiss on his head. She passed the ipad back to Jason and smiled. It had been a week since they had spoken with John Schaeffer, and he had kept up his end of the bargain. She whispered to Jason, "Did they find out who the original leak was?"

"Linchpin's assistant – Schaeffer said they found him in Peru. He's agreed to testify in exchange for immunity. Probably Witness Protection is his next stop, I'd imagine."

Kate was thankful that she chose to pass the file off and stay out of the limelight. If Schaeffer hadn't been so interested in credit, that would have been her family needing a new identity.

Kate heard a door knock, and "Hello!" as Kate's parents entered. "We thought we'd share our pizza with you. Is that alright?" Kate's mom said.

"Grandma!" the boys shouted with glee, jumping up from Kate's lap and untangling themselves from the cover. They ran to Grandma and Grandpa and gave them good long hugs. The six of them sat down to dinner and laughed at all that had happened the past weekend.

"Do you think we are going to have any more of those strange MAG guys hanging out at our house?" Kate's dad asked.

"Absolutely," Kate said, "those guys are ok in my book."

"Wow, look how far you've come. From preppie to prepper," Jason teased.

"I wouldn't go that far. I'm just smart enough to find the crazy preppers in a pinch to help me out," Kate joked back.

Landon tugged on Kate's clothes, "Momma, can I have this?" he asked, waving a paper in his mother's face.

Kate looked down to see it was the menu from the Chinese restaurant, the Red Tiger. She must have laid it on the counter when she unloaded the backpack. "Yes, my red tiger may have that," she answered.

"Where did you get it, Momma?" Landon asked.

Kate smiled. "From the Red Tiger restaurant. And you know what? The Red Tiger helped keep your mom safe this weekend."

Landon ran to his brother with glee. "Look, Logan, I saved Momma!"

Both boys ran to Jason. "Daddy, red tiger saved Momma!" Logan shouted.

"Yeah, Daddy, I saved Momma!" Landon echoed. Kate's smile couldn't have been any bigger.

"It's hard to believe you packed up a 30/30 and then ran from the cops," Kate's mom said.

"I think it's harder for me to believe that I escaped!" Kate laughed.

"Momma, you are a super-cool secret agent!" Landon said.

"And you're pretty," Logan added as he kissed his mother on the cheek.

Did you hear that? You are a super-cool, pretty, secret agent," Jason said.

Kate's heart was full.